Michelle,
Thank you for being
a reader and for giving
a sweet review!
Love,
Robin

See You in 48

Robin Densmore Fuson

Robin Densmore Fuson
Psalm 91

Forget Me Not Romances, an imprint of Winged Publications

Thank you to the other authors in Forget Me Not Romances for your encouragement and acceptance as part of this fantastic group of writers.

Winged Publications

ISBN-13: 978-1-965352-00-7

A depraved, determined murderer, a committed and equally determined detective, and a woman who dreams dreams. Robin Fuson has put together a psychological whodunit that ends with a twist and will keep you reading long into the night - with all the lights on!

Linda K. Rodante, author of Christian romantic suspense novels in The Dangerous Series and The Spiritual Warfare Series.

You intended to harm me, but God intended it all for good. He brought me to this position so I could save the lives of many people.” (Genesis 50: 20 NLT)

Chapter 1

Sirens blazed on the black SUV, which skidded to a stop by the yellow tape partitioning off the two-story house. Recently promoted Detective Dustin McCall climbed from the driver's side and followed his mentor and friend, Detective Jim Marlow, to the waiting officer.

"Dustin, it's all yours. I'm just an extra pair of eyes and a listening ear. You've earned the right for this to be your case."

Dustin nodded, took a deep breath, and stepped around Jim to the policemen, who held the tape for them to stoop through. As a boy, Dustin used to like the cheery color yellow. After crossing that line too many times, the color now sickened him.

Death waited behind the tape.

Inside the house, Dustin locked eyes with Officer Kent. "What we got?"

"Sir, I've not seen anything like this. The bathtub fell through all the way to the basement. Unbelievable."

"Accident?"

"Not by my standards. Thought you two should take a look."

Jim raised a palm. "Kent, I'm an extra from here on out. Direct everything to Lead Detective McCall."

Kent grinned. "Yes, sir."

Dustin nodded, taking the mantle and slipped on his detective persona. He tried to keep his eyes on everything at once. The smallest detail might be a clue. "A tidy, uncluttered house. Nothing seems out of place. Any evidence of a break-in?"

Kent shook his head. "We didn't find any. Windows and doors were locked up tight."

Dustin kept his cowboy hat on and pulled on booties over his boots. The extra-large NBR nitrile gloves snapped into place over his sizable, well-worked hands. Kent led them down the hall to a door under the stairs. "The body is in the unfinished basement."

Dustin went first but stopped at the first glimpse, mentally recording the whole scene. After a long moment, he took the rest of the wooden stairs to the concrete cavern where the distinctive but familiar smell met his nose—death.

In the back corner piled the devastation—a fractured bathtub, holding the broken and bloody body of a substantial man atop soggy building debris. Dustin winced, sighed, and shook his head. "What a way to die." He glanced at an officer snapping pictures and another one taking a slow approach, recording the scene in a video.

The concrete, still wet and pooled in places, showed the trail of water to the drain, now clogged with bits and pieces of splintered wood and insulation. Dustin took care where he planted his feet, not wanting soggy booties. A gaping hole above displayed the tub's descent through two floors from the remains of the master bathroom. After the videographer finished capturing the scene, Dustin climbed upon the pile and tilted his head to look through the hole. "It's unnerving to see the unscathed side of a cabinet and part of a framed mirror. Like a Ripley's Believe it or Not exhibit."

Marlow deepened his furrowed brow. "Exactly. I've seen a lot in my day but this wins the award for most bizarre."

The coroner arrived and Dustin pulled him aside. "Walter, take it nice and slow."

Walter nodded and gingerly waded through the rubble to the deceased. He bent over and picked up a book, then handed it to his assistant who passed it back to the detectives.

Marlow read the title. "*Frankenstein*. Interesting read. Did it fall through because of the crash or did our victim carry it with him?" He slipped it into an evidence bag.

Kent opened his notebook and rattled off, "Colin Raffey, sixty-four, divorced, no children. Arrived home yesterday from a three-day business trip to New York." He looked up. "What I wanted to show you detectives is this wood here." He shined his flashlight up into the hole. "The subfloor, braces, and hardwood appear to be cut. Here,—here,—here,—and—here. All this would've collapsed when enough weight landed on them. I checked upstairs. There, too. And take a look at these plumbing pieces, also cut." He stooped and used his pencil to move them for a better look. "I'm guessing they're from the drain on the tub."

Dustin and Marlow both squatted next to Kent. With his gloved hand, Dustin picked up a piece of PVC, showed it to Marlow, and nodded. "The evidence so far shows a planned murder, not a fateful accident. Thanks for calling it, Kent. Send officers to canvass. Someone must have seen someone or something out of place."

"You got it."

For the next hour, Dustin directed what needed to be bagged and taken in for evidence.

Rows of monitors filled the room. Each group live-streamed multiple areas from a particular address. The man captured the events from ten residences. He liked round numbers, so when one expired, he added the next. His three-person team did a good job, making it possible for the man to enjoy his creativity by watching it unfold as if he were there. This way, he disassociated himself from the crimes but still enjoyed his passions.

One by one, the new bank of monitors went live. The perfectly hidden cameras gave him an amazing wide-angle view.

He diverted his attention to another cluster of screens. One of his team members installed wires and pulleys. His fingers twitched with anticipation as his masterful plan unfolded on an array of screens before his eyes.

Victoria Miller woke to the soft voice of Fredrick Harper, PsyD. "Victoria, how do you feel?"

Victoria blinked a few times. "Much better. Thank you. Yes. The pain is gone." She moved her neck, stretching it from side to side to be sure. Perfect.

"After my car crash, my personal experience with hypnosis as a means to alleviate migraines proved the best option. I want my patients to enjoy relief as I did. My thoughts are your treatment has been successful and you're almost guaranteed to be migraine-free for a considerable time. Even for a redhead." Dr. Harper chuckled at his own wit. "Let's make your next assessment for three months from now."

Victoria smiled. "Sounds good." She lowered the footrest on the comfy faux-leather recliner, stood and stretched. "Thank you. I feel relaxed and pain-free." Wanting to dance through the door, instead she sashayed out to the reception desk. Head held high, back erect, with a gleeful smile on her face, she made an appointment, then strode to her car.

The sunshine didn't cause daggers in her eyes and temples. She beamed. To be on the safe side, she slid on her designer sunglasses—a splurge, she admitted—but the dark polarized lenses helped with the sun and driving. Her reflection in the rearview mirror told her the expense was worth every penny. Not wanting bed hair, she fluffed the back of it out then pulled her white car into the Durango traffic.

She loved living in the mountain town, but during tourist season the traffic became annoying. Bicycles, motorcycles, vehicles, and pedestrians vied for the road and walkways.

She turned the soft-rock music up and swayed her upper body to the beat.

Right now, nothing could dampen her mood.

Migraine-free. A year ago, her pain and the sunlight made it impossible for her to drive to appointments so her friend Malena had to chauffeur her around.

Now behind the wheel and pain-free, she spoke to the Bluetooth, "Call Malena Campbell."

Soon her friend's voice answered, "Tori, how did your appointment go?"

"Amazing. How I feel is excited for a pain-free future. I know you don't believe in hypnosis, but I'm proof it works."

"I'm skeptical but glad for you. Just be careful. You've lost so much weight besides the headaches."

"Weird, right?" Tori snickered. "I'll take the added bonus."

"You don't think…"

"No, I don't. I only asked for migraine relief. My outlook has shifted, so I'm taking better care of myself. The main thing is I've not experienced migraines for the last eight months, except for the occasional one-day affairs. It's a new record."

"Well, I'm happy for you. I've watched you suffer for a long, long time, even in college."

"I'm sorry we kept the dorm room dark most of the time. You were so accommodating. Malena, seriously, thank you for not abandoning me and for going the extra mile." Tori giggled, "No pun intended, driving me everywhere I needed. You're an amazing friend."

"We should celebrate. Jalyn would love to see you and hear the news. She's been praying for you. How about the three of us do lunch?"

"Set it up."

"Great. Talk to you in a few."

Tori ended the call. Excited and feeling

marvelous, it amazed her she experienced no side effects. A shadow flickered over her soul and she frowned. Except for being tired. As if she hadn't slept. A few weeks ago, the disturbing dreams started. She chewed on her lip. Maybe she should've mentioned that to Dr. Harper.

The most difficult part, the part Dustin always dreaded, was over. No amount of training prepared him for those encounters. Early in his career, he took over the deed himself—notifying loved ones. At the station, he took off his shades and climbed out of his SUV. The sunny day contrasted with his heavy heart. He scanned the cobalt sky. No clouds. No wind. Hot and dry. Nothing moved.

In the office he shared with his partner, he took off his hat and put it atop the coat rack. Marlow appeared massive, leaning back in his chair, feet propped on his desk, all six-feet-two stretched out. "How'd it go?"

"Typical." Dustin settled into his comfortable office chair. "Raffey's parents are in their late eighties. I told them the news, slow and gentle. Waited until the tears dried a bit then sat with them while they showed me pictures of their son." He filed the memory into the myriad of other such files. The stunned, devastated faces burned into his brain, and would remain as scars for the rest of his life, joining all the other families of the numerous victims. Dustin couldn't help but keep a file for them in his mind. Sometimes they crept into his thoughts and even haunted his sleep. The families and the victims were why he worked tirelessly to bring the perps to justice.

"Raffey's parents are finding it difficult to understand their only child from all appearances died in his bathtub. I told them we're investigating the structure to determine why and how it happened."

Dustin's mind went back to the moment he gave them his card. He told them to call him if they thought of anything. "Besides my card, I gave them one for the grief group. I encouraged them to talk about it. Hope they do. Parents aren't supposed to bury their children." He shook his head.

Marlow lifted his feet off the desk. "I checked the ex-wife's alibi. She's remarried and living in Canada. So we can scratch her off the list."

"Got it. Any other suspects? Kent find anything from the canvass?"

"He's still at it."

The text came in on both their phones. "Ready? Walter's waiting for us."

Dustin led the way to the morgue where they put on gowns, gloves, and bootees. Observing an autopsy, although interesting, was part of the job Dustin disliked. Walter's team used Neutrolene to eliminate the smell of death, but visuals and sounds still embedded themselves into his psyche. The body underwent swabbing for evidence and each wound was examined through a magnifier. Saws whined and organs were weighed as Walter spoke into his mouthpiece to record the proceedings. Would he ever get used to this?

The next day, although he already knew what it would say, Dustin read the coroner's report stating death resulted from a broken neck and spine, with head trauma from the fall. He studied the familiar sketch Walter used to mark where bones were fractured and ribs punctured lungs.

"Too many Xs and circles." At the bottom, Dustin read the list of ruptured organs and turned toward Marlow. "Unbelievable. If Raffey somehow survived, he would've required years of corrective surgery and rehab."

It sickened him. He scanned the rest of the document, which indicated no toxins and no injuries prior to death. Dustin muttered. "A healthy person, although overweight, snuffed out in his prime. Why?"

"That, my partner, is what you need to find out." Marlow clicked a few keys on the keyboard. "The canvass of the neighborhood for suspects and clues yielded zilch."

Dustin ran a hand over his face, which needed a shave, and squeezed his cheeks. Officer Kent had done a thorough job heading up the canvass and background. "Raffey seems to be clean. All of his family and friends agreed Raffey was a kind, decent man. Other than his occasional business trips, he appeared to be a homebody. He puttered around in his garden and read from his extensive library—mostly classics and botany." Dustin made some notes—check the local nursery and stores—talk to his coworkers and boss—see if he had any enemies. He got up, trekked across the room, and knocked on Marlow's desk. "Let's go for a ride. We can grab lunch on the way."

Chapter 2

Darkness shrouded the room except for the flickering of the screens. The man needed to experience the environment of the next victim as much as possible. He stared at the dark shadowy shapes outlining the door and staircase, wishing the scene was in color. Using a joystick, he rotated the lens to see the rectangular box at the bottom of the stairs.

His thoughts went to the lengths he'd gone in order to procure the species in the cage at the bottom of the stairs. A few months ago, a picture of a dude with at least a dozen snakes caught his attention. The recent hurricane had created the exact piece of the puzzle he needed. Water rising caused critters of all kinds to move to higher ground. The joker in the picture found snakes in the attic and his kids' clubhouse in the tree. A sizable sum of money enticed the dude to put one of the adorable vipers into the special container and send it to the PO Box.

All roads leading to him were untraceable. Cash only. The PO Box listed a person long dead. IP addresses scrambled all over the globe. Burner phones. An incredible amount of forethought went into his obsession. Soon, the next play would unfold. The alarm sounded. Show time! Giddiness oozed like molten lava through his soul.

The man moved the lens for the best view and kept his fingers there, ready to follow the movements. He rasped, "Curtains up," and quivered with anticipation.

On the screen, he watched the door open. A hand reached out to flip on the light. At the same time, the woman's front foot snagged a wire which began the sequence of events.

The pulleys went into action—tugging the rug from under the woman's bare feet.

Feet sprang into the air.

Head slammed down on the tread—blunt contact with each one.

Arms flaying, she slid, as on a slide, crumpling in a heap on the concrete in the basement. Simultaneously the other pulley opened the cage to ensure death.

"Yes. Genius. Better than I thought." He congratulated himself.

The man watched the snake's head when it came out, tongue first. He loved every minute of detail—giggling at the multiple strikes on the quivering victim.

After the deed, he turned his attention to another bank of monitors, where sunrise awakened an older woman to her morning routine. After pouring a Bloody Mary into a ruby red goblet, she shuffled, drink in hand, to her deck where the bubbling hot tub waited. She slipped off her robe onto the chaise lounge and stepped into the swirling water.

He should kill her for no other reason than no woman over the age of eighty should wear a bikini.

Sipping and soaking for a half-hour, she climbed out to sit in the sun and read a book.

"Your routine will be interrupted soon, you old bat."

"The glass found under the fragmented flooring and bathtub showed the perp gained entry through the basement window. A few of the pieces have clean breaks. The killer is sophisticated. He or she didn't break the glass, but scored it and left it inside with the blue note taped on.

SEE YOU IN 48 HOURS

What's that supposed to mean?" Dustin studied the papers in front of him on his desk, then peered over at his partner who held duplicate copies.

"No noise." Jim Marlow tapped his finger on his nose.

"Exactly why the neighbors didn't hear anything until the final crash. Unbelievable." McCall shook his head. "You're relaxing in your own tub when the bottom literally falls out of your world."

"Tough break." Marlow took a drink of his coffee and winced. "No alarm system to cut. No dog. Not even a doorbell camera. Not that it would've made a difference. The perp used the best method for entry. The egress window's substantial size made it possible to bring in the saw used to make the cuts to the subfloor and the rest."

"A free-standing tub made of porcelain." Dustin flicked his finger against the photo. "Not all houses come with those. Most are built in with tile and everything. This one only needed the drain and floors cut. No one checks the drain on their tub before they plug it and start the water. I will from now on. Raffey had no clue when he climbed into his death trap. How did the perp know what kind of tub? He must've been in the house prior. We need to get service, repairs, painters—" Dustin scribbled as he spoke, "—anyone who's been in the house. The perp must be a math genius—physics prof or an engineer of some sort—to figure the weight allotment before the tub fell through. Maybe a professor at Ft. Lewis?"

"That's an idea to follow." Marlow huffed. "There's still no suspect or motive. He's clean. Not even a traffic ticket. No relationship issues at work or places he frequents. His divorce seemed respectful and pleasant. She fell in love with another guy and moved on. You said he didn't do much on the computer. Blimey, the VIC's only passion was flowers." He tossed the picture of Raffey's garden in front of where the window had been removed. "Rocks to walk on. Not even a footprint. Dear Lord, I want this solved before my retirement."

At a pulsing restaurant, Victoria waited for her friends, Malena and Jalyn. The comforting aroma of fried food caused her mouth to water. She yawned for the twentieth time and took a long drink of the strong coffee, hoping the caffeine and sugar would kick in. Muffled voices rose over the music vibrating through the speakers.

Victoria scanned the room. She saw Malena

heading her way, followed closely by Jalyn. Victoria grinned at how different her two friends looked—Malena, the statuesque brunette, and Jalyn, the pretty redhead. Their faces lit up when they saw her waiting for them. Victoria grinned. This should be fun.

Malena beamed at her and bent for a hug. "How's my dear friend? You look tired."

"I am today, but you're as chipper as always. Hi, Jalyn, it's been a while."

Jalyn also leaned in for a hug. "Good to see you, Tori. I'm glad we could get together."

"Please." Tori waved her hand toward the other chairs.

"I haven't been here for a while. I'm glad you thought of it, Malena." Jalyn took a seat across from Tori.

"This is perfect. A beautiful day and my favorite women together for lunch. It can't get much better." Malena grinned.

After a few minutes of scouring the menu, they gave their orders to the server. Jalyn unfolded her napkin and placed it on her lap. "I love the weather this time of year. I don't mind evening rainstorms, since the flowers need it, but I love the dry and sunny days! Have you seen the flower baskets and planters on Main Street? They are gorgeous."

"Yes, our town is enduring and amazing, but that brings out the tourists." Tori pursed her lips. "They're everywhere and parking is a nightmare. Watch them drive." Tori shook her head. "Incredible."

"It was much worse when we had the great race." Malena nodded and beamed at Jalyn.

Jalyn grinned back. "For sure."

"That's when Jalyn's amazing husband came back into her life. He was one of the cyclists that year they raced the Narrow Gauge train."

"I remember the event. The explosion too." Tori shuddered and frowned. "I seem to recall a maniac who tried to kill someone."

Malena nodded. "Don't you remember? Jalyn had a target on her back. You can read about the whole adventure in the news online. She's a reporter for The Herald."

"I don't think we were friends then. So you're the one who was in great danger. I'll have to look up the articles online to refresh my memory. Are you okay?"

"I'm fine." Jalyn leaned back as the server placed food in front of her. "Thank you." She turned her attention back to Tori. "Anyway, I agree, the traffic can become intense around here."

The burgers stalled their conversation while they took those first scrumptious bites. Victoria cut her burger in half and divided her fries for the take-home box she'd asked for in advance. Voices and clanging dishes faded away while Victoria devoured the first bites of the loaded cheeseburger with melty cheese, tomato, onions, lettuce, and pickles. The special sauce gave it a little kick. "I'm glad you two didn't order salads. I needed this. Comfort food is my best friend right now."

Malena put her hand on Tori's forearm. "Still not sleeping?"

"I climb into bed and fall right to sleep. But when the alarm goes off, I feel like I've just crawled under the covers. I'm exhausted, as if I worked out at the gym all night."

Malena rubbed Tori's arm. "You said you were experiencing bad dreams?"

"Yes. But they're all fuzzy. I can almost remember them, but it's as if a switch goes off and they fade away." She forced a laugh. "Crazy, right?"

"I dream, but seldom remember them when I wake up. Are you still teaching?" Jalyn popped a fry into her mouth.

"Yes. Kindergarten. I'm glad we're on break." Tori glanced past Jalyn to the T.V. screen in the bar area where a local news crew stood in front of a house draped with crime tape. She stared. The blood drained from her head, and she couldn't breathe.

"What's wrong?" Jalyn asked.

Tori took quick short breaths. "I've seen that house before."

Jalyn turned around to face the screen.

Malena asked, "When?"

"In my dream. At least a snapshot."

Jalyn swiveled back. One eyebrow rose to her hairline. "I'll move closer and see what they're reporting." She went to the high-mounted television. After a few minutes, she returned. "Seems a murder occurred there. Something about a fall down the stairs and a snake."

"Oh no! Not another one with a murder." Tori buried her head in her hands. "Why am I seeing these?"

Malena put an arm around her friend. "You've seen other houses?"

She nodded. "A few. Crimes also happened at those."

Jalyn put down her fork. "How long has this been going on?"

Tori scrunched up her face. “A few days.”

“You said another one with a murder.” Malena stirred her iced tea.

“Yes. Do you remember the one where the guy died in his bathtub? I envisioned that house too.”

Jalyn leaned forward. “Malena, don’t you think Tori should talk to Dusty?”

Malena nodded. “Yes.”

Tori folded her hands in her lap. “Isn’t Dusty your boyfriend? The one who’s a detective?”

“Yep.” She grinned. “He’s now lead detective. Detective Dustin McCall. I love the sound of it.” She patted Tori’s arm again. “You should tell him about those vibes, visions, dreams, or whatever they are. Maybe if you tell him, he can get there before the crime.”

“I didn’t think about that.” Tori pushed her plate away. “The visions frighten me. They’re not real clear, kind of like an old black-and-white silent movie. What do you think? Have I become some sort of clairvoyant?”

Malena and Jalyn exchanged glances.

Tori splayed her hands. “Do you think God is showing me so I can help these poor people?”

Chapter 3

The scrambling news crews shoved microphones in Dustin's face. How had they gotten wind of this so quickly? He waved them off and followed Kent into the crime scene.

Inside the door, they booteed and gloved up. "How'd they hear about this?" Dustin thumbed to the mob out front.

"A tipster called the station and gave the address. Called it murder."

"They give their name?"

Kent nodded. "Yeah, Anonymous."

"Figures. Get their call records, but first—lead the way."

Kent went through the kitchen to the basement's open door and pointed inside. "A wire seems to have been attached here on the casing."

"Another body in a basement?"

"Yep. This case is also a strange way to die. From what we surmise, the resident and owner of the house, Jane Dixon, stepped on the landing, and the rug took her down the stairs, where she crumpled at the bottom."

Dustin shrugged. "People fall down the stairs all the time."

"Yes, but the wire she tripped on triggered a sequence of events. And who has a rug runner on the stairs? I think the perp brought it, clipped a wire to it, then attached it to a pulley system. The poor woman hit her head at least once on the stairs then the other pulley opened the cage. To make sure there's no doubt it's murder, the perp attached a note."

Dustin reached for the plastic bag containing an identical blue notecard which said verbatim what the first one did.

SEE YOU IN 48 HOURS

Dustin whistled. "Not funny. What else do you have?"

"Animal rescue is here catching the snake."

"Snake? You've got to be kidding me." Dustin's heart raced. He backed up. His eyes darted from the floor to the stairs and his hands turned clammy. "Why would she have a snake?"

"I'm thinking she didn't. Perp put it there to kill her."

"Okay." Dustin kept his size elevens two feet from the threshold, put his hands on each side of the doorframe, and leaned in to look down. A small open cage stood next to the crumpled body. A bunched-up rug lay partially under her. He scanned around the basement as far as possible without passing the threshold.

A loud voice floated from the cavern. "Officer, we got it. A beauty of a pit viper, ah, and hopping mad at the moment. A cottonmouth." A guy came into view carrying the squirming reptile clutched in a long chrome device with pinchers imprisoning its flat head. He shoved it into the cage and clanged it closed. "Do you want this serpent, or do you prefer me to take it off your hands?"

Kent looked at Dustin.

The snake repeatedly struck the metal, trying to get to the captor. "Take it." Dustin squeezed his eyes for a moment. "No. We need to check out the cage and whatever evidence the snake has. Give the whole thing to the forensic team."

The guy nodded and moved up the stairs with the cage.

Dustin scooted back into the kitchen behind the island, with his eyes glued to the basement door. The guy came up with the critter and took it outside. From the kitchen window, Dustin watched him transfer the snake to the forensic team, who tucked it into the sealed van. His voice came out in a croak. "Are we sure there was only one?" He cleared his throat.

"Pretty sure. Cage is small. The woman seems to have been dead for over twelve hours. Her husband, Bob Dixon, is on the way back from an ophthalmology conference in Florida. He was already in flight when we arrived. His itinerary and flight number were in her date book on the desk. Lucky for us she was organized. We didn't have to unlock her phone. He'll be met at the gate." Kent tapped his notebook.

Dustin steadied his voice. "Who found her?"

"Cleaning lady, Carmen Pérez. Cleans twice a month. She's in the living room."

"Is she good, or do we need to interview her later?"

"She's holding up and we have her info."

"Tell them I'll be there in a moment." Dustin went to the basement door and scanned the lower area once more.

Dustin headed to the living room. A wiry older woman sat on a gray sofa, wringing a tissue in her hands. A tangy scent of cleaning products hung around her.

Dustin nodded and showed his badge. “Ms. Pérez, I’m Detective McCall. Can you tell me what happened, starting with when you entered the house?” He sat across from her on a smaller matching sofa.

“I unlocked the door like I do every time.” She lifted her key. “I went to the kitchen to fill the dishwasher and noticed the open door to the basement and the light on. That’s not right. It’s always shut. All lights off when I come. I don’t clean basement. So, I look in. Mrs. Dixon on the floor. Puffy…swollen. Bloody.” She shuddered. “I ran to my phone and punched 911. I didn’t go down or touch nothin’.” Tears started. She made the sign of the cross.

“Thank you. I’m sorry you found her. I’m sure Mr. Dixon will contact you, and if we need you again, we’ll give you a call. You can go home now. This officer will escort you outside.” He pointed to the female officer. “Through the mob of reporters. Please don’t talk to them.”

Dustin stood there for a moment before braving the basement. Why did it have to be a snake?

The television news showed the house where yellow tape blocked the entrance while the media person rambled on about the couple who lived there.

Microphone in hand, she speculated, creating more questions than her lame answers as to what transpired inside.

The watcher appreciated their take on matters, but they didn't have a clue. He snickered and toasted them with a sip of his tangy medicinal cocktail.

Another monitor grabbed his attention. The most unfortunate senior detective's unresponsive body jerked when paramedics attended to his heart attack. Marlow needed to be taken out. McCall was the one he wanted to match wits with, but Marlow stood in the way and should've retired as instructed.

He'd keep Marlow's address live for a while. The man drew a line through the address from the house on the T.V. and selected another from the list he'd amassed. Tonight he'd add it to the bank of monitors at the time of activation.

The murderer hated the lull as much as he hated odd numbers but not as much as he loved his process and accomplishments. To prevent the odd numbers, he kept the cameras live inside the house where the detective spoke to the cleaning woman. This morning, as if on cue, she'd been right on time. Her reactions to the discovery excited him.

The fact they found the viper so soon was regrettable. Time belonged to him. Time to watch. Time to enjoy the scurry and search. From what he observed, the buffoon of a detective had a fear of snakes, maybe a bona fide phobia. He guffawed as he imagined what it would be like to sneak into McCall's house while he slept and put snakes all over his bed. McCall could die of fright. A perfect way to get even. Glee quivered through his body. Should he add him to his list?

An ingenious pulley system. Dustin spent a couple of hours calling stores that sold that brand from Utah to Kansas and Wyoming to Texas, with no luck.

Hands laced behind his head and legs stretched onto the desk, Dustin stared at the eight-foot glass board in his office, holding names, dates, and crime scene photos. His gut screamed serial killer even though there were only two murders.

Only two. His stomach knotted. Two too many. The victims' pictures smiled at him from the board. So far, he couldn't find connections between them. Basements? A guy who kills people in their basements? In strange ways? Coincidence? How were they linked?

Mr. Dixon didn't give them any leads. They were happily married. Got along well with neighbors. Financials in order. No large life insurance payout. They had two kids attending college in California and Texas. All of them were devastated.

Dustin picked up the blue card left at the scene and spoke to the empty room. "No prints on this ordinary, unlined index card. All the stores carry them, even this color—City Market, Walmart, Walgreens, heck even Amazon. It's a dead-end." The first card warned of 48 hours and the second murder occurred within the time frame. The second card stated the same. Precious little time to prevent the next murder. Who? Where? How?

He checked his watch again. Jim never failed to come in early.

Dustin dropped his feet to the floor and again flipped through the victim's date book. Something niggled in his brain. There must be a connection.

His cell phone interrupted his concentration. "McCall. What?..." He bolted out the door. "Not Marlow. On my way."

Chapter 4

At the hospital, Dustin found the parking lot full and pulled into a spot reserved for law enforcement. Keeping the motor running, he sat to collect his thoughts and calmed himself before he saw his partner.

The door to the entrance swished open, and cool air hit him. He took off his cowboy hat then strode to Intensive Care, where he found the room of his friend and mentor. After saying a quick prayer, he knocked on the slightly open door, identified himself, and pushed it open.

Monitors with numbers and squiggly lines on their screens met Dustin's eyes. His gaze traveled along the wires to the man in the bed. Dustin took a deep breath, put on his encouraging face, then approached Jim. "Hey, partner. What gives? You takin' a break 'cause these cases resemble the rat in a maze with no seeming way out?"

"Ha. Right. Trade you places anytime." Jim's voice sounded weak.

"What happened?"

"Heart failure. Seems the ticker almost ticked its last. Surgery is scheduled for the morning to put in stints." Jim shook his head. "Insulin got in my system."

"Insulin? You're not diabetic. How?"

Jim shook his head. Closed his eyes. "Someone administered it."

Chills ran through Dustin's body. "You're saying you were targeted? Someone wanted you dead?"

Jim opened his eyes and stared at Dustin.

Dustin pulled out his phone and ordered a 24-hour guard for Jim.

"Any idea who did this?"

"That's the worst part. I don't know."

"Worst part? You could've died. Where were you?"

"Downtown. In the crowds. Someone bumped into me. Felt a sharp prick but didn't think about it. A few blocks later, I started sweating, stumbled into a store, and said, 'call 911.'"

"Are you kidding? Sounds like that spy back in '78 that was injected with ricin. We're in a flippin' spy novel. How'd you get involved?"

"I should've heeded the warning."

Dustin frowned and posted his hands on his belt buckle.

"In my home office…top drawer…threat note." His voice was so weak Dustin leaned close to hear.

Dustin stood straight. "I'll find it and get to the bottom of this."

A knock on the door caused Dustin to turn. An officer poked his head in, and Dustin went out to give him instructions. "Someone wants Detective Marlow dead. Do not, under any circumstances, leave your post. Need something, call it in. I'll be here for a few minutes. Go get coffee. Food. A magazine. You know the drill. Be prepared for the rest of the day until relieved."

"Right."

As the officer left, Dustin spotted a familiar face and waited. Jim's married daughter, Jenny, scurried up the hall. As she drew closer, he noticed deep worry lines marred her beautiful face. Wrapping her in a bear hug, he whispered, "He'll be fine. Your dad's in excellent hands."

She stepped out of his embrace and nodded. "Daddy doesn't have diabetes. How'd this happen?"

"I'll find out. I promise. In the meantime, a policeman will be stationed right outside his door. Don't worry. Your dad is safe. How's your mom?"

Jenny swiped at a tear. "Mom's a wreck. Torn apart. She's taking care of Aunt Karen in Nebraska but wants to be here and there. I told her to stay. I'll keep her updated. Maybe this happened for a reason. We knew Dad's heart was weak, but we didn't know to what extent. The insulin made his heart worse. Now he needs to have surgery. If the paramedics didn't get there in time…Dustin, I almost lost him."

"I know." He gave her another hug. "I'll tell Malena and I'm sure she'll call. Do you need me to talk to anyone else? Do you need anything?"

"Just Malena." She shook her head and went into the room to sit with her dad. Dustin followed. He watched the scene before him—Jenny's brave smile as she held her father's hand. Jim's loving eyes fixed on his daughter's face. Who wanted this amazing man dead? Enemies? Jim? None that he could think of.

Dustin moseyed up to the bed. "The surgeons will fix your heart. Probably make it better than before. You got this." Dustin patted the older man on the shoulder.

"Hey, God's got this. Right?" He included Jenny in his encouragement.

Jim nodded. "Of course. Just not my preference or timing."

"Can I get ya anything?"

"No." He took a deep breath, winced, then turned eyes of steel on Dustin. "Yeah, you catch the miserable good for nothin' creep who's plaguing our town. Sooner, not later, so get outta here."

"You got it. See ya tomorrow. But first, let me pray with you both." He placed a hand on his friend's arm and the other on Jenny's shoulder. "Lord, please fix this old man's heart and get him up again to be the burr under my saddle real soon. And Lord, bring comfort to those who love him. In Jesus' name, Amen." He opened his eyes. "I'll take you riding as soon as you're up to it."

"I'll hold you to it."

He gently patted Jim's shoulder and left. The officer sat in a chair beside the open door with a stash of stuff to occupy him for a while. Dustin smiled, happy to see him ready. "Detective Marlow's daughter, Jenny, is inside with him. Don't hesitate to call for any reason."

"Rodger that."

Dustin nodded and headed to the exit, where he put on his hat and sunglasses.

In the SUV, he slammed his fist against the steering wheel. "Why, Lord? Jim's a great guy and the best partner. This town needs him. His kids and his grandkids need him. I need him. Who had it in for him? Why didn't Jim tell me about the threat?"

Dustin started the car and drove straight to Jim's

home. He found the key and entered. After a quick search, he held a blue notecard in gloved fingers.

Get off the case. Retire or you'll regret it

Same kind of card as the ones at the crime scenes, and the techs needed to go over it for any evidence. Why threaten him off the case?

On the way to the office, his mind went over the crime scenes and the evidence. A wave of doubt crowded in. "Lord, am I up to solving this case by myself? You know who the murderer is. Direct me to him before anyone else gets hurt. Show me what I'm missing. There has to be something. Some evidence overlooked." His mind went to what troubled him. "What's with the calendar book?"

Inside headquarters, Dustin rounded the corner and almost collided with Malena. "Whoa." He caught her shoulders. "Looking for me, beautiful?"

Her eyes lit up and her lips parted in a captivating grin, causing his heart to race. "Yes. I brought someone to see you." She stepped away and grabbed a woman's hand. "Dustin, this is my friend Victoria. She might be helpful to your cases."

Dustin frowned. "What cases?"

"Those terrible murders that are on the news. I assumed you were handling them."

"Let's go to my office." He led the way. As fast as a maglev train, he shoved all the papers and photos into a folder and flipped the board so the women wouldn't view the gruesome photos. He took off his hat, hanging it on the coat-rack, then raked his hand through the creases left in his hair.

"Have a seat." He motioned to the only two chairs, closed the door, and perched on the edge of the desk. "What do you want to tell me?"

Victoria, the pretty redhead, spoke first. "Malena talked me into coming." She looked at Malena then down to her tight-fisted hands in her lap. "Don't think me a whacko, but I get these visions about the houses where the crimes have happened."

"What do you mean? Dreams? How often? Before or after?"

She lifted her head and frowned. "Before the crime. Sometimes dreams and other times I see them in my mind when I'm awake. At first, they're hazy but as soon as I see them on the TV screen, they become crystal clear. It's like looking through poorly adjusted binoculars, then the lens flips and all of a sudden the image is clear."

Dustin glanced at Malena then turned his attention to Victoria. "Okay. How often does this happen?"

Victoria shrugged. "I get shadowy images for a few days before, then like I said, wham, it's clear when I see it on the screen."

"Well," he rubbed his chin. "When you see the fuzzy image, try to draw it. Or look for an address or something particular on the image. Then give me a call." He handed her his card. "Thank you for coming in."

He pushed off his desk. "I'll walk you both out."

He avoided Malena's eyes and opened the door for them.

So far, things had gone almost flawlessly. Almost. Marlow should be dead. Not the man's fault—only unforeseen timing. A *fault* in this tennis match, of sorts. Marlow managed to find someone to call 911, the paramedics happened to be close by, and arrived too soon. The old detective should've heeded the warning and stayed out of the game.

He sipped from the straw in his drink and refocused on what turned out right.

News that Marlow lay in the hospital gave the man chills. Marlow out of the way. Superb. On each hand, his fingers rubbed against his palms over and over.

Because of what he'd overheard, he'd need to make adjustments. The man shrugged. He always devised a backup if his plan went awry. He'd change workers for the next few jobs.

A thought came to him. He tilted his head and giggled at his brilliance—use the problem as a misdirect.

The man worked best in the dead of the night.

He loved that saying.

While most of Durango slept, he spoke soft seductive words into the device, giving directions for the next stage of his diabolical scheme.

Keep the law on its toes. Overloaded. Easier to get away with things when they didn't have time to follow leads. Confident of his perfect plan, he also wanted the extra assurance of an overworked law-enforcement team. Thus Marlow was taken out.

He picked up another device and gave further

instructions.

Next, he needed to change out the addresses on a row of monitors. One useless. Dead. A new one soon to go live, well, for a short time anyway. He crackled. A dead address meant a dead body. The man liked that idea. He scanned the remaining names on the kill list.

If they only knew.

Malena placed her arm around Tori's shoulders. "Don't worry, he didn't shut you out. He told you what to do to help him. You can do that. He's a busy man, but he did hear you."

Her eyebrows furrowed. "I sounded too weird to him. I can't help what I see."

"I know, but I'm glad you told him. Now you understand what to concentrate on in the vision. Make notes or draw a picture of the house. What it looks like." Malena offered Tori a most reassuring smile. "He'll be able to use what you give him."

After a quick hug, Malena climbed back into her car. She waved goodbye and drove home.

At her place, Malena kicked off her shoes and called Dustin. "Why did you dismiss her like that? Tori isn't crazy. She volunteered to come and tell you. It took a lot of convincing to get her to see you."

"Babe, she didn't have much to tell. An image that gets clear when she sees it on TV? How does she know what she saw in her vision was the same thing? That's why I asked her to draw it. Give herself and me more information. Malena, you know I'll take any lead anytime. I just need more to go on. If she sees an image and can identify it, we'll rescue the target and capture the perpetrator before it takes place."

"Okay. It just seemed you were brisk with her—a jerk of a detective instead of the sensitive, open and kind man you are." Malena heard him click his tongue. She stopped pacing, perched on the couch, and softened her voice. "How's the case coming?"

"It's frustrating. Not enough leads. But we'll get them." He cleared his throat. "Hon, um, sweetheart, I need to tell you something."

Fear clutched her heart. "What?"

"Jim's in the hospital. He collapsed in a store and he's scheduled for stint surgery tomorrow morning."

She bolted up. "Oh no! Why didn't you call me or tell me earlier when I saw you?"

"Because I knew you'd rush over and there isn't anything you can do. Jenny could use a call, though. Do the thing you do. Make the family feel better. He seemed fine but tired when I saw him. Jim's getting the best care at Mercy Medical."

"You're right. I'll call the family." She sat back down.

"Surgery is at eight."

"Okay, I'll pray for him. Hey, thanks for being on the job. It makes me feel safer."

"Sure, babe. I'll talk to you later."

After calling Jim's family, Malena phoned Jalyn to catch her up on Jim.

Jalyn answered on the fourth ring. "Hey, how are you?"

"Doing okay, but Detective Marlow is in the hospital."

"Oh no. What happened?"

"Heart surgery. They'll put in stints." Malena shook her head at the fragility of life.

"I'm sorry to hear about Detective Marlow. I remember him being nice to Adam and me during that time my life was in danger. From what I hear, he's taken Dustin under his wing."

"He did. Dustin looks up to him. Jim's been giving Dustin more of the caseload and put him as lead on the new ones. Now, I guess he's got 'em all." Malena blew air. "Anyway, I called Jim's family. His wife is out of town taking care of her sister, but I talked to Jenny and scheduled meals to be delivered and sent flowers."

"You're so thoughtful. I bet they appreciate it."

Malena took a deep breath and brightened her voice. "On another note, I took Tori to see Dustin today. He asked her to draw what she sees and then call him. I think these cases are getting to him. He's got that look."

"Ah, the one where he looks at you and you feel he might drill a hole into you?"

"Yep. That one. It's intense. That's for sure." Malena giggled. "But cute too."

"Ain't love blind!" Jalyn laughed.

"Of course. But seriously, I hope Tori can draw them or get clearer visions of what the houses look like. Then Dustin can stop this horrible person. I pray that's the last."

"Do you think the same man or woman did the murders?"

Malena shuddered. "Well, I hope there aren't two killers on the loose. I'm already frightened. Dustin said there weren't many leads. Let's keep these families in prayer and pray that Dustin gets a break to catch him or her."

"Durango's not a high-crime place. Why all of a sudden?"

Chapter 5

Victoria woke up in a sweat. She scrambled out of bed. At the desk, she found a pad of paper. With swift steady hands she drew the fading vision—a multi-story building. The phone read 2:07 AM. What should she do? The detective would be asleep. What if there was another murder? She paced and worried over it for fifteen minutes.

Picking up the phone, she tapped Malena's name. After the fifth ring, the groggy voice of her friend answered. "Tori?"

"Malena, I'm sorry to wake you, but I don't know what to do."

"What's wrong?"

"I had another vision and drew the place like Detective McCall asked."

"Why didn't you call him?"

"He's probably asleep." Tori sighed. "And I'm worried it could be nothing."

"Trust yourself. Call him. You won't know until he investigates."

Tori's mind raced. "You sure he won't be angry?"

"I know if you don't call and it's a lead, we'll both be angry."

Tori pleaded, "Maybe you should call. Then if he thinks it's a viable clue, he can call me."

Malena groaned. "For you, this time I will. I'm sure he'll call right away."

Tension eased, and she looked at the screen, realizing Malena hung up. Tori took a deep breath, slowly releasing, "Good ol' Malena."

~  ~

Dustin answered on the first recognizable chimes of the ring. "Malena, you okay?"

"Yes. Sorry to wake you."

"Not even home yet." Dustin fisted his eye.

"Dusty, you need to sleep."

"Right. What's up?"

"Tori called and said she's had another vision and drew it but she's afraid to call you."

He puffed air out his cheeks. "Text me her number."

"Did you sigh? Don't be frustrated. She's doing what you told her to do."

"Yes. But she called you instead of me. That's a problem. She shouldn't have disrupted your sleep."

"Don't be harsh with her. She's frightened too."

"Tell me a little about her. Does she have any issues? Health? Financial? Relational?"

"She was a fantastic roommate in college."

"Oh. You've known her that long? Why didn't I know?"

"Tori's had some physical issues with migraines, which kept her inside. She attended our church before you came along. Used to be overweight so you might not recognize her as the same person. Tori went red instead of blonde. She decided it gave her power." Malena giggled.

"She probably wanted to be strong and gorgeous like you but couldn't pull off the brunette."

"Right. I don't think so. Most likely she's rocking the Jalyn look. Anyway, Tori's a schoolteacher. She overcame migraines through hypnotism by Dr. Harper. Rents a house in the cute suburb where Ted lives."

"Hypnosis? Interesting. Married or single?"

"Single."

"Okay. Text me her number."

"Dusty?"

"Yeah, yeah. Nice and sweet."

"Thanks. Good night."

"Night, Mal, I love you."

"Love you too."

He called Tori, then drove over to her house. The sketch showed a brick multiplex with large outside areas built against a hillside. He knew of a few scattered in and around Durango. When the sun came up, he'd drive around to see if any matched the drawing.

In the spotless room, the man wearing a pressed button-down shirt sat in his padded chair, the only lights coming from the glare of the computer screens in front of him. He grinned when the pen scratched across a name on the list. How he loved that simple yet fulfilling motion. Another dead. Exhilarated, he recalled the wrinkled old body pulled from the scalding water. He watched it all.

The old woman did her predictable routine—reclined in the water and sipped her morning shot of vodka. Only this time, the goblet had been laced with a tasteless drug. Soon her eyes closed. Her hand holding the goblet relaxed. The glass dipped in the water and swirled. Hours upon hours he watched her life slip away. Time meant nothing. The kill meant everything. The jets of rotating water pulled her from the edge to float like a water lily.

Later, an officer appeared at the side of the hot-tub then scrambled to reach her carotid, to detect a pulse. Ha! His face said it all.

None.

The detective and coroner arrived at the same time. He wished he could've heard the conversation. Although state-of-the-art, the inferior camera made it impossible to read lips. The slump of McCall's shoulders, when he found the blue card, shouted—bested.

"Fifteen-love." He tipped his drink, toasting himself.

Reminiscing finished, the man looked at his list.

He sobered.

His list grew shorter. The fun would eventually come to an end.

Or would it?

Three days passed since Jim's surgery and Dustin entered the hospital room, longing to go over the case. The patient sat on the edge of the adjustable bed, dressed in blue and gray lightweight athletic pants and matching hoodie, waiting to be released.

Jenny, curled into a chair by the window, waved and went back to her tablet.

He clasped his friend on the shoulder. "You look great. Getting out today, I hear."

Jim grinned. "After the paperwork is complete."

"Remember I told you about the woman who thinks she's psychic and claims she sees the residence of the VIC before the crime?"

Jim nodded.

"Turns out, she and Malena were roommates in college. She gave me a sketch of a condominium building. I drove around but didn't find it, so I staked out her house for days, thinking she'd led me to another killing. Nothing. She got another 'quote unquote vision' and again I assigned officers to stake out a different house. I'm wasting resources for nothing."

"You're following leads. Thant's what you have to do. You'd get crucified if you didn't and another crime happened."

"Unfortunately, a murder did take place but not at any of the stakeout houses. We got a report of a female floating in her hot tub. When I drove up, I took another look at the sketch. The woman drew it down to the bushes on the outside of the complex. The hairs on my arms stood up. Somehow, she's involved, or she's a visionary. It's sticky with her so close to Malena."

Marlow frowned. "Don't like that. Who found the body?"

"A realtor saw her from a window of a townhouse higher up on the ridge." Dustin handed Marlow the folder and pointed at the photo of the woman in the swirling water.

"How'd she die?"

"Boiled."

Marlow jerked his head up, almost dropping the folder. "What?"

"Walter said high doses of gamma-hydroxybutyric acid—GHB or as you know its street name, liquid ecstasy—were in her system. That combined with alcohol, she passed out fast and long. As she slept, the hot tub boiled her alive. We checked the heating system and the regulator had been disconnected. The condo is fairly new but the heater was old and not self-contained, or perhaps replaced with an older one. We're looking into it."

Marlow whistled. "Same perp? Not a basement this time. Any connection? Did you find a note?"

"Yes. I think…"

Jenny stepped up, hands on her hips. "Dustin, Dad, must you? You did have heart surgery and were poisoned, remember? I thought you'd go ahead and retire. Please Daddy, don't do this." She swiped the file from her father's hands and shoved it against Dustin's chest, papers scattering.

"Sorry, Jenny." He clasped the file. "You're right. Old habits." He bent to retrieve the file's contents. "Your dad's smart. I wanted another set of clear-thinking eyes." He stood and tapped the file into his palm.

"Well, you'll need to find someone else." She hugged Dustin. "I know you don't mean to hurt Dad, but he needs to heal before being worked up on a case." She motioned to the door.

"Your daughter's right." Dustin shook Jim's hand. "Thanks, partner, for mentoring me. I've got this. You concentrate on getting well." He kissed Jenny on the cheek. "Take care of him. See you both later. Malena and I'll make dinner for you once you're up to it to celebrate your recovery. We'll keep an officer on you until this is ended."

Dustin spun on his heel and left the hospital, kicking himself for his lack of empathy. The case got to him and he wanted a seasoned detective to go through it. Jim's health didn't allow him to help Dustin now or maybe ever. Before climbing into the SUV, he tugged off his jacket. Leaning on the frame, he rested his head on his forearms. Dustin missed his partner and wasn't sure he could do it alone. Once behind the wheel, he slammed the door shut and started the car. Nope. Not up to it. But like it or not, it was all on him. He cranked up the AC and headed to interrogate the house cleaner.

For the second time, the suspect, Carmen Pérez, sat in an interrogation room. Dustin watched her face and mannerisms while he questioned her. "How long have you worked for Regina Billings?"

"Five years. Why?"

"We found her dead."

"Dead?" The shock written on her face seemed real.

"You appear to be the central link in a chain of

dead bodies. What do you have against these people?"

Tears gushed from her eyes. She covered her face to the point he barely understood her. "I don't do this horrible thing you say. Never! They nice people. No. Can't be dead." Her shoulders shook.

Dustin hated himself but continued the badgering. He needed answers. "You had access. Keys to each person's home. Show me the keys."

Carmen lifted a hefty ring out of her bag and dropped it, clanging onto the table.

"Point out which ones."

Using a finger, she moved them. "They have names on them. Here's the ones."

Dustin nodded and turned to Kent. "Dust these." Kent lifted the ring with a pencil and placed it on another table, then left while Dustin continued with the suspect. "You're the only link between them. Give me the list of other people you work for so we can see if they are also one of your victims."

Carmen moaned. "It not me. My list on phone."

"Show me."

Her quaking hands prodded the device. "My jobs." She shifted the phone to face Dustin.

Dustin used his phone to take a picture of the list.

Kent entered and brushed powder over the keys to retrieve any prints.

Against all odds, Dustin hoped to catch a break and extract clear prints of anyone other than hers. "For now, you're free to go. When he's finished, Officer Kent will take you home. Don't leave town." Since he didn't have a warrant, he couldn't detain her or keep the phone.

Chapter 6

Dustin sent officers to patrol the neighborhoods of the list of residents Carmen Pérez cleaned. He sat in his office reading over the reports and evidence again. The managing company of the condo complex where hot-tub victim Regina Billings lived reported the heater was a different brand and age than the others in the complex. Pictures taken at the scene showed tool marks on the fittings. His tech crew told him the regulator wires were cut out of the circuit.

"The perp is going to a lot of trouble in these killings. Did he think we wouldn't discover this?" Dustin mused to the empty room. He always processed problems by talking out loud, and he missed bouncing ideas off of Jim and discussing theories with him. Who could he get for a sounding board?

A knock on his open door caused him to look up. "Yep?"

"Got a body."

Driven to the monitors to stroke his obsession, he

forgot his elixir. The concoction couldn't be neglected. It necessitated going back to the kitchen.

The schedule alarm already sounded. He screamed, "Never late. Never late."

Sweat broke out on his forehead.

What should he do? He couldn't go without it, but he might miss the show.

Panic attacked.

His hands trembled.

On the trek back to the refrigerator, his brain screamed, What a fool. You didn't plan well enough. Why did you let yourself oversleep? You rushed and forgot. How could you? Stupid. Stupid. His fingernails dug into his palms.

Eight minutes lost.

After retrieving the jug and returning to the monitors, his quaking fingers moved the controller to view his next masterpiece. Maybe he arrived back in time.

"No!" Anguished cries spewed out. Deep in the bowels of his domain, no one could hear him. The screen showed the male body already on the floor. The man didn't get to watch the episode leading to death. He pounded his fist on the armrest. "No." A stupid mistake causing him to miss all the fun. Tears of frustration slid down his scruffy face. To calm himself, he sucked from the thick straw protruding from his drink.

While he watched, paramedics arrived. The frantic movements told a story but they didn't lift his mood.

He switched his attention to another address, where the monitors showed his worker wearing a headlight as he labored in a cramped space, affixing a large cylinder to bypass the water heater.

The man's heart rate slowed as anticipation mounted. "Good. That's right." His installer wiggled back out of the space and darkness enveloped the screen. He sneered knowing the water heater sat in the tiny attic above the garage. This gave him an advantage over the victim. Odds were the cylinder would remain hidden and the rescue would turn into a long, drawn-out process.

He refocused his attention on the finished murder and observed the detective squat to peer at the corpse. The man scooted closer to watch every move McCall made.

He noted the time. McCall arrived at the crime scene too fast. How?

Energy flowed through Tori, and wanting to celebrate, she called Malena. "You want to go to dinner and catch a movie? Or we could get delivery and hang out."

"You sound chipper. What's up?"

"I don't feel sleep-deprived and I haven't received strange visions for days. I feel like I could conquer the world. Want to go hiking Saturday?" Tori put the phone on speaker and touched her toes to stretch her legs.

"Goodness. Sounds like you have your zing back. That's terrific."

Tori heard in her friend's voice the encouragement and it buoyed her energy even more.

Malena continued, "Sorry, but I can't go tonight.

I'm supposed to meet Dusty for dinner. We haven't had a date for ages since those freaky murders started. Saturday may work. I'll let you know after I see the new customer for her fitting tomorrow. She might need altering, and if it's a crunch, I may be sewing at the boutique."

"Of course." Tori did a few squats. "Maybe I'll swing by your dress shop to see your new arrivals. If I can't be walking through the woods, running my fingers on some silk will be a nice diversion. I want to do something, get out—anything. I've been afraid to go anywhere since all this started."

"How about Sunday after church? We can grab a bite."

Tori stood. "Hm. I do need to get back into church. Sure. Is it still 9:00?"

"Yes. Want me to pick you up?"

"That would take you out of your way. I'll get there, I promise."

"Super. I'll save you a seat and a donut."

"Ha Ha. No donut. A seat and coffee will be fine." She jogged in place. Tori had sworn off donuts or anything with empty calories. She loved her new trim figure, another bonus of hypnosis.

Malena laughed. "How many jumping jacks have you done this morning?"

"None. Only a few squats and now…I'm running… in place."

"I'll let you get back to it. Maybe I'll see you Saturday and for sure on Sunday. Bye, girl."

"Right. Bye."

Tori ended the call, pocketed her phone and jogged out the front door. She paused to tap in the code on the fancy door handle before jogging up the sidewalk.

The paramedics packed up and left, leaving Dustin stunned. Ted Wilson had died with the EpiPen inches from his leg. A mocking blue card held the same message.

SEE YOU IN 48 HOURS

"How did this happen? What's with this box of peanuts?" He almost threw it at an officer. "Find out where it came from. Why did his device fail him?" Dustin's fists clinched. The desire to punch something, to throttle the perp, almost overwhelmed him. He unclenched his hands and his jaw then lowered his voice. "Sorry, guys. I knew Ted. Please find explanations and evidence fast but be thorough." His officers and the tech personnel were on top of things. Another person died, but this person, Ted, happened to be a friend from church. He closed his eyes, took a deep breath, held it a moment, then slowly blew it out.

Now he needed to go comfort Ted's fiancée, Willow. Malena, also friends with the engaged couple, would be devastated. He told himself to settle down for Willow's sake, for Malena's, and for him to use rational thinking.

Dustin found Willow on the back patio sitting with an officer.

Her head down and shoulders shaking, she repeated, "Why? Why?"

He wanted to know too. Lord, help me say the right thing and help me find out how and why this happened.

Dustin nodded at the officer, who stepped away into the background, then he took the vacated seat, reaching for her hand. "Willow." He shook his head. "I'm so sorry."

Her tear-stained face turned toward him. She flung herself into his arms. "Dustin, I…I…" she sobbed, "I fou….found…him. Oh, Lord, have mercy!"

Dustin recognized the sign—too distraught to answer. "Let me take you to Malena." He helped her up and half carried her through the gate to his vehicle, avoiding the house.

He got her in and buckled. Dustin hurried to the driver's side while his mind taunted him. Your friend died on your watch. Pathetic. You let it happen. Leaning against the hood, he gathered his thoughts and composure as he surveyed the street and the commotion around the officers. One officer rolled out crime tape—the yellow taunting him, "Ha! Another one you let happen."

Dustin tore his eyes away and lifted them to the cloudless, deep blue sky. God. Help me! I can't catch a break in these cases. My gut and the blue card tell me Ted is one of those. There has to be a link. Something to point to the guy. Four, Lord, four dead people. How many more have to die?

Phone in hand, he made a quick text to Malena. Bringing Willow. Something happened. Need tea and tissues. Malena told him many times that tea comforted. Well, she and Willow would need gallons of the stuff.

Dustin scraped his hand over his face and climbed into his SUV. He turned off the emergency light and flipped a U-turn, heading for Malena's boutique.

Pounding the pavement, Tori rounded the corner to see flashing lights of emergency vehicles. Her feet slowed as she surveyed the ruckus. As the house came into view, goosebumps erupted on her skin. "I know that house."

She sped up and arrived after a black SUV did a U-turn heading in the opposite direction. Her shoulders slumped. "I'm too late to stop it. Again."

Tori looked at the numbers on the house and frowned. The address didn't evoke any memories of a party or friends living there. She massaged her temples. There's no reference to why she knew this house. Yet, it's a crime scene. Why was it familiar? Why didn't the house appear in a vision?

Should she let one of the officers know? Why would it matter? She hadn't prevented whatever happened inside. Maybe it was just a burglary? She huffed. Just—a burglary. Absurd. A few months ago, that would've been terrible and frightening but a burglary brought—relief.

Stay and try to find out what happened? Wait until she heard the report on the news? Go to Detective McCall? With what?

Tori turned around, checked her watch for her athletic progress, shrugged, and walked back home. All energy—drained.

Chapter 7

The familiar cell chime brought Malena to read Dusty's text.

"What in the world?" A cloud descended, giving her a heavy heart. She slid back from her sewing machine and went to the kitchenette to fill the electric pot, praying as she worked. "Lord, I don't know what's going on but I've got a bad feeling. For Dusty to bring Willow, it's bad. Real bad. Help me to know what to say and do to help Dustin with whatever he needs. And, Lord, please comfort my friend. Only You know."

She grabbed two mugs, dropped Earl Grey tea bags in, added a squeeze of honey, and poured in hot water. Malena carried the two mugs to her sitting area. The smell of the potent brew with the scent of oil of bergamot comforted her. The feminine decor normally cheered her, but now she dismissed it as frivolous. Her mind and heart were filled with prayer for her friends, Willow and Ted.

Malena met Dusty and a tearful Willow at the door. Questions rambled around in her head. "Come in. Willow, honey, what happened?"

Her friend went into her arms. "Ted. He's gone."

"What? No. Not Ted. Oh, sweetie." Did she mean

left? Or—dead? She peered up at Dustin who wore his cop face. Dread filled her and she knew the answer. He'd tell her what he could.

Her attention back on Willow, she said, "Let's sit down and you can tell me about it, or we can just sit." Malena led her to the loveseat and sat next to her with her arm around her shoulders. She handed her a tissue and waited.

The soft click of the door closing let her know Dustin returned to the investigation.

Willow sniffed and murmured, "I came over to help him paint. We are—" She squeezed her eyes shut, "*were* getting the house ready to sell. We decided we would live in my townhouse after we got married. It's closer to work. I found the door unlocked and entered. I called his name. He didn't respond. I went into the kitchen and found him lying—" A sob escaped, and she hiccupped. "On the floor. Rash. Swollen. Not breathing."

Frustration radiated through Dustin. He had to keep it in. Showing it or letting it out in anger would impede progress. Everyone on the force did their best to scrounge up evidence and suspects. He rocked back in his office chair. The comforting creak reminded him of when Malena gifted it to him. On his birthday, she'd wheeled it in with a bright red bow. His sweetheart knew his affinity for well-crafted antiques. Dustin reveled in the solid oak office chair. He ran his hand over the well-worn silky armrest. If only life could be that smooth.

The cardboard box retrieved from the crime scene sat on Dustin's desk. He already knew the contents but he dug through the box of real peanuts, not the Styrofoam kind, searching for something, anything. Nothing.

He closed the flaps and ran his finger over the label—Ted's name and address, neatly typed. No postmark or other carrier markings. Hand-delivered. He hoped the second canvass of the neighbors yielded a witness or camera angles of the package being dropped off. Dustin visualized Ted picking up the box at the door and going to the counter where he took his pocketknife, slitting it open. They found the knife beside the opened box. Nothing inside but the nuts. Ted, intensely allergic to peanuts, would only need to inhale the dust from them. In distress, he would've shot himself with a dose from the ever-faithful Epi. Dustin put the box down and picked up Walter's findings. One of the hardest things he'd done—witness a friend's autopsy. Those images—forever branded into his mind.

He tried to picture the deranged mind behind this killing but couldn't and shook his head.

The evidence showed the EpiPen didn't misfire. It and Ted's supply of other medicinal pens contained water. Someone had painstakingly taken the device apart, emptied its contents, and refilled it with tinted water. Simple food coloring that anyone could get at a grocery store—not that anyone could see the liquid inside the pen. An artist with dexterity put it back together and made it appear to be straight from the pharmacy. Deliberate. Cunning. Diabolical.

Now, his friend—fiancé, son, brother, and all-around good guy—lay in the morgue. Why Ted? He didn't pay to have his house cleaned, so that ruled Carmen out, at least on this one. Or was it some sort of diversion? Why would anyone take such great pains and means to kill a diversion? No, somehow the target landed on Ted's back. Dustin took a deep breath and blew it out in a slow flow.

Earlier, Willow texted Dustin the code to unlock Ted's phone and Dustin searched through messages, emails, and the calendar. Working overtime, social media tech personnel scoured through the sites Ted frequented, coming up empty. He slid all the items into a file box with the name Wilson and added the date.

Dustin tore his mind through the other crimes. The results of the DNA collected at the bathtub and stair/snake murders hadn't come in yet. Those took precious time. Fingerprints all belonged to the victims.

He hoped and prayed something would come from the hot tub murder. They traced the heater to a pawnshop in a small town in New Mexico. The camera feed in the store's black and white images showed a slight man in a hoodie wearing a surgical facemask. His skin appeared to be light. Not much help there. The owner didn't remember him purchasing the odd device. So far, everything led to a dead end. Dustin's body clinched tight and ready to explode like a Jack-in-the-box.

He picked up his phone and tapped Malena's number. It rang several times. He sighed and dropped his phone on the desk. Dustin ran his hand through his hair.

"Dusty, you all right?" Malena's voice jarred him. He jumped up, raced to the door, and pulled her into a bear hug. He swung her into the room and kicked the door shut.

She giggled.

He stifled the giggle with a kiss.

After the long one, he said, "Thank you."

Encircled in his arms, Malena leaned back, searched his face, and frowned. "For what?"

"Coming in here looking and smelling like you do. I needed that. I need you. How are you?"

She cupped his face. "I'm fine. Don't worry about me."

He searched her eyes. "Hard not to after Ted. How's Willow?"

"A mess. Have you found out anything?"

He puffed out a breath. "The Epi didn't work. Been tampered with."

Her lips pursed, eyes grew huge, and she shook her head. He led her to one of two chairs facing his desk. "Babe, I tried calling you. I need to see Willow and give her the information. Want to go with me? Also, I won't be at church tomorrow."

"Of course I'll go with you. Dusty, don't you need a break? You canceled our date and now you think skipping church will catch the murderer?"

He slouched into the other chair. "I'll think about it. Have you eaten? I'll buy you a burger on the way to Willow's."

"Bribe all you want. Not going to church is between you and God. Take it up with Him. Yes, I'd love something to eat. Ready now?"

"Sure thing." He stood, put on his hat, pocketed his phone, and grabbed his sunglasses.

The man sneered as he watched his brother. "Hurry up. I can't be late again today."

"Okay. Trying. Can't rush. No. Must be right or—or you get mad."

His brother's whiny voice grated on his nerves. He despised him. Was repulsed by him. Needed him. "That's enough. Put it in place, so I can get to work."

"Done." His brother stepped back.

The man nodded. "Do your chores. I expect everything put away in the places we marked. If it's not perfect, I won't be happy. You can make the soup you like but clean up afterwards. There should be a delivery today. I ordered a new puzzle that will keep you busy for a long time."

"Yay." His brother clapped his hands. "Th-thank you."

"Good. Mother can help you. Can you remember all that?" He counted on his fingers. "One, put everything away, like I've shown you. Two, cook soup. Three, clean the kitchen. Four, a new puzzle is coming today." He saw understanding in his brother's eyes then glanced at his mother, who nodded. The man headed for the hand-print-activated elevator, which took him down into his world of electronics and murder.

Sitting in front of the rows of monitors, he grinned. He regarded his reflection in the one dark screen. Sharp features on a clean-shaven face. Intelligent eyes. Every button fastened on his crisp white shirt. The soft wool gray cap sat straight on his bald head. He checked the watch—on time and ready for the day.

The room temperature he kept at a cool sixty-five degrees. This room and what unfolded on each screen delighted him. He lived for this. His world. Here he could forget his past and the two people three floors up.

One monitor showed yellow tape flapping in the wind. He watched it whip back and forth, up and down. Might an end get pulled away and the tape flap in the breeze? Someone would have to fix it. Soon.

Although difficult, he redirected his attention to the other screens on that row. Room by room. Furnished but empty. One room held paint buckets and tools. Days before, he watched the couple interact with each other as they painted the walls. The way they took breaks, gazed into each other's eyes, and kissed made him angry. His mind went back to when he enjoyed female company. He remembered everything about them. Their softness and scent. Voices and laughter. The man clenched his teeth and shut off the monitors of that address. How he wished he'd witnessed the peanut guy die. Too late. He arrived too late and didn't see the woman find him either, although he caught a glimpse of her at the edge of the screen while the paramedics tried to revive Ted. Then they led her away. The outside camera showed her sitting in a chair on the patio. The cameras followed McCall's movements at the body then outside comforting the pretty fiancée.

The man spoiled that romance. A cackle spewed out. No doubt they realized he ruled supreme and domineered everything.

Chapter 8

Malena saved two seats, one for Tori and the other in hopes Dusty arrived for Bible study. Beside her sat Jalyn and her husband, Adam. He held her hand and they whispered cheek-to-cheek, evidence of much love flowing between them. A few days ago, they celebrated their first wedding anniversary. Thrilled for them, Malena silently chuckled then sent up a prayer for their love to continue unhindered.

The teacher stood, gave a few announcements, then opened in prayer. "Turn to the ninth chapter of John and let's see who is to blame for a man born blind."

Victoria bustled through the door. Malena smiled at her and watched her make her way to the seat reserved for Dustin. A glance around showed the full room contained only one empty chair on the other side of Tori. Malena looked at her watch. Her shoulders slumped. He wouldn't be coming.

Malena needed a distraction, so she settled in, and enjoyed the study followed by the uplifting worship service. The two hours seemed to fly.

Afterwards in the parking lot, she said to Jalyn and

Adam, "Tori and I are going to lunch. Want to come?"

Jalyn smiled and nodded. "We don't have any plans."

"Are you sure? Adam, you'll be the only guy."

"I'll be the envy of all others. It's not every day I'm blessed with the company of three beauties."

One of Adam's friends hollered across the parking lot. "Hey, Adam. Would you like to be the third? We're scheduled to do a three-on-three but our third backed out. We reserved the court."

Adam looked at Jalyn, who chortled. "Go. Then we can talk, girl talk." She playfully shoved him.

He kissed her cheek. "Love you. Have fun."

"Come back in one piece."

He jogged over and jumped into his truck, drove to the other guys' vehicle, spoke out the window, then wheeled out of the lot.

At the restaurant, servers carried dishes ladened with food to tables. Delightful aromas mingled with chatter as they were taken to a table near a window. Malena peered out the window at hanging baskets infused with color. The fuchsia, orange, and white flowers glowed in the sunshine. Malena let the beauty calm her soul, then turned her attention back to her friends.

Jalyn settled in her chair. "How's Willow?"

"She's lost. The love of her life snuffed out in seconds." Malena fiddled with her napkin, loss hitting its mark, dousing the moment of peace. What if this happened to Dusty? Her mind went to the devastation she witnessed in Willow's tortured eyes. She'd feel the same. "I don't know how she is going to cope. Every time I talk with her, she's crying. Her parents are trying to convince her to move back to Wisconsin. I told her she should go for a long visit, at least. Ted's parents want him buried in Arizona where the family owns plots. I told her I'd help her with a memorial here if she wanted one. She can't make up her mind on anything."

Jalyn put her hand over Malena's. "I've been praying for her and the families." Malena smirked then immediately chided herself. It's not Jalyn's fault. Why show anger to her?

"Where did this happen?" Tori asked.

"At Ted's house." Malena frowned. "Tori, it's a few blocks from your place. You know them?"

Tori shook her head. Her eyes grew huge, her hands flew to cover her face, and she groaned.

"What? Are you okay?" Malena put her arm across her shoulders. "What's wrong?"

"I think I saw the crime scene."

Malena gasped. "Another vision?"

She shook her head. "I took a run and came upon it. The house seemed familiar but I didn't see it ahead of time in my head."

"Did you tell Dustin?"

Another slight shake of her head. "What good would it do?" came her muffled reply.

"Tori. It's not your fault. Look at me."

After a long moment, Tori wrapped her arms around her chest in a protective embrace. Her face appeared blotchy, brows furrowed, and she chewed on her lip. "Why didn't I see it beforehand? It's my fault. I should be able to control the visions. I see them, then I don't. Think I'm going out of my mind. I scheduled an appointment with Dr. Harper. Maybe he can help me pull them up."

Jalyn leaned forward. “You’re not going to get hypnotized again, are you?”

Tori nodded. “It’s the only way to figure it out. Maybe I’m suppressing something.”

Lines appeared on Jalyn’s forehead. “I’m worried. I wouldn’t want someone inside my head. Malena, what do you think?”

Malena pursed her lips thinking the same thing but conceded the obvious. “He helped her with the migraines and her eating habits. I offered her a donut and she emphatically denied wanting one.” Her eyebrows lifted. “Maybe it won’t hurt?”

Jalyn shook her head and rested her hand on Tori’s. “I’m glad he improved those things but having him help with an intangible thing? How will you know he did? Are you going to ask him to find visions in your head that you don’t know are there? What if he put them there to begin with?”

Malena gasped. “Can he do that?”

“Oh, surely not.” Tori waved a dismissive hand. “Anyway, he can’t see me for a few weeks. Unless it’s an emergency, he’s booked. I didn’t ask what constituted an emergency.”

His gravelly voice lowered in pitch and the man whispered in the mouthpiece, “Good job. Go back to sleep. You’ll wake refreshed, ready for your day, and the events of this night will be erased.” He spoke a few keywords and made clicking sounds that the ears and brain were receptive to hear and obey.

The man sneered as he watched the person turn on his side. He watched until he knew by the rhythm of breathing his subject slept.

Another job well done. He wanted to pat himself on the shoulder. He knew how to use his voice and inflection to garner respect and obedience. The man's skills were exceptional, his greatest asset—his masterful brain. No one came close to his intelligence. Hadn't he received awards and recognition for his brilliant inventions and patents? Of course.

He surveyed the monitors and gloated on the state-of-the-art voice-command system. "I needn't lift a finger for the world to obey." He laughed then switched on both the police scanner and the emergency dispatcher to capture the wave of excitement about to unfold on one of the screens he witnessed.

A male voice from dispatch said, "911, what is your emergency?"

A frantic female voice answered, "My husband. Hurry! I can't get it open. He's in agony. He's dying. Hurry!"

"Open what?"

"The shower. Hurry! It's killing him!"

"What's your address?"

The man spoke the numbers at the same time as the distraught woman, then he crowed. His laugh turned into a coughing fit.

After catching his breath, he sipped his drink. The words being spoken angered him and he cursed. He'd missed most of the exchange. Although he knew they headed to try to rescue the man. Of course, no one would be able to reach him in time. Not even close for that matter. He held in the glee for fear of coughing again. Instead, he swigged from his theriac potion and delighted in the drama of the frantic woman trying to crash open the shower door.

Racing to the car, Dustin prayed the emergency team would get there in time. After the hot tub victim, Dustin patched into 911 and listened to dispatch. Time was of the essence and he needed to stay near the radio.

Forty-Eight hours raced by and he couldn't afford to go to church. Didn't this new emergency prove it? Driving like a tornado through a Kansas prairie, his flashers on, he argued with himself. No. The call didn't come in until after church. Dustin could've attended. His vehicle cleared the intersection and he stomped on the gas. These murders were all-consuming and he got little sleep. The constant cup of coffee in his hand kept him going.

One common denominator—Carmen Pérez—he once pegged for the murders, but Ted didn't have any cleaning service. Hers were the only fingerprints on the keys. Yes, almost too clean. Not a smudge under the clear fingerprints. A cleaner by profession, Carmen appeared neat and tidy. Maybe she cleaned the articles in her purse often. He made a mental note to check as he took the next corner fast, jarring the SUV. Besides, he didn't think she possessed the skill set to figure out the complexity of the crimes.

Dustin shifted his focus to the list he had burned into his head of eggheads and brainiacs he needed to interview. Someone with powerful gray matter designed the murders. No guns or knives were used. Nothing typical. Two of the eggheads dropped off the list because they were out of the country.

Dustin arrived right behind the EMTs. As he jumped out of the SUV, he heard a shout, "Someone shut off the water." Running to the garage, he found an officer climbing up into the crawlspace. Dustin followed.

"What? How? The valve is already off." The officer pulled his hand away.

Dustin wiggled around him. "What's that?" he pointed to a large cylinder.

"I don't know."

Dustin turned the valve. "Turn everything off that's connected to water lines." They both scanned the space for any other spigots. "Why are we turning off the water supply?"

"Detective, it's barbaric. The guy is melting in the shower. It has to be some sort of acid. We can't get the door to open. The woman slammed her vanity chair against the tempered glass to no avail. If she had shattered the glass, she would've been burned too." The officer shook his head and clambered down the ladder.

Dustin stood there in dumbfounded silence.

He scanned the small room. A speck of blue poked out from under the cylinder. Dustin, already gloved up, pulled the piece out from under the cylinder. His gut knew what he'd read.

SEE YOU IN 48 HOURS

Chapter 9

The rows of monitors with ten addresses flickered with visions that pleased the man. Important things happened at each. Even the mundane became important. He detected emotion from the occupants in both magnified and slight movements, also facial expressions.

The lower right row held his address. Cameras were installed in each room of his home and around the perimeter of the house including the half-mile driveway that twisted up the mountain. A buzzer sounded when a vehicle traversed the first curve alerting him—much safer than a booth with an armed guard that would bring unwanted attention. Everything they wanted was delivered. The occupants of the house never left the premises.

In one screen, he made sure his brother and mother didn't get into mischief. Right now, they sat at a ten-foot by eight-foot folding table that held all eighteen-thousand pieces of the puzzle he'd bought them. The puzzle depicted the Sistine Chapel. They finished the border and a few other globs of light-colored images locked together to form the giant picture. Other similar shaded pieces were grouped and scattered around the massive outline. That should keep the family busy for a long while. If they were lucky, all the pieces would be accounted for in the end. He uttered a derisive chuckle.

The television in the room where they sat showed reruns of *Gunsmoke.* He didn't mind them watching the western he found comic. He preferred movies of the mind. *Silence of the Lamb, Zodiac, Inception,* and *Shutter Island* were some of his favorites. On this mission, he didn't have time for movies except for the ones at the addresses in front of him. Those "actors" didn't have a script but they played their parts to perfection.

The monitors for the murder in progress showed people in hazmat, scooping the remains of the man out of the shower. He guessed the suits to be a level 2 at the very least. Another camera revealed someone also in a complete suit with a face guard in the attic taking out the canister, which should be nearly empty by now. He tipped his drink toward the monitor. "Cheers."

~  ~

Unbelievable. Over the years, Dustin investigated fierce crime scenes but this one took him to the outer limits. What kind of twisted mind killed people that way? It went beyond reason. The maniac needed to be stopped. The evidence gathered from all the scenes sat on his desk or up on the board.

Dustin endured a massive headache and a churning stomach from all the coffee he ingested to keep awake the last forty hours. Living at headquarters or on a crime scene took its toll and he wished this all a horrid dream. He didn't want to sleep, for the nightmare of the crime scenes came alive more vivid and skewed than the real thing. Plus the real ones came every forty-eight hours.

No time to sleep.

The beautiful weather outside beckoned him to ride across the mesa with Malena next to him on her lovely horse Annie. He hadn't been on his horse, Champion, for too long. Good thing his groom kept him exercised.

He shook his head to rein in his thoughts. He must be tired. These people didn't deserve to die, let alone in these ways—innocent people doing routine activities.

He stood, went to the board, and tapped a picture. "Taking a bath and falling to your death." Dustin stepped to the next image. "Going to the basement to exercise then tripping, sliding down the stairs, and getting bitten by a deadly snake." He shuddered and went to the third victim. "Pouring a drug-induced drink and stepping into your own hot tub to be boiled." Ted's smiling face filled the fourth spot. He took the picture off the board, holding it a moment. "My buddy. How insane to open a package and die from anaphylaxis." He put the picture back and swiped at his eyes and his face. "Now a man locked in his shower to be liquefied by acid spraying instead of water." From his desk, he picked up a portrait to add to the board. He wrote *BURT SWANSON* above the smiling man with Kim, his wife.

Deputy Kent strode in. "Sir. You need to watch the news." He tapped the tablet in his hand. Dustin watched his own face appear on the screen then heard the news anchor. "Is Durango safe with this man heading the investigation? His partner, Detective Marlow, is out on sick leave, and rumors say he's slated to retire. Does McCall have the wherewithal to find this person or persons capable of killing people in rapid succession? So far, no arrests. Folks keep your doors locked. The security companies are now kept busy installing cameras and alarms as people are afraid to be in their own homes. 911 dispatchers are going nuts with reports from frightened people calling about the slightest noises around their homes. Detective Marlow, come back to put us at ease and solve this case."

Dustin raked his hand through his typically close-cropped hair, now long overdue for a haircut. "Thanks, Kent."

Kent stepped to the door and turned. "You'll show 'em, sir. You'll catch the killer. I've no doubt."

Dustin didn't think so. He'd become sluggish. He didn't have leads. The newscaster was right. Marlow would've solved it and had the murdering creep behind bars by now. He dropped his face into his hands. "God help me. I need a crumb, anything." The plea went to the One who knows everything. Opening his eyes, a small book caught his attention—the appointment book of the second victim.

He eased into his desk chair and picked up the book, flipped to the date of her demise, and went back over the previous month. Then he skipped forward to appointments not fulfilled. "What? That's recurring." He flipped pages back and forth as excitement mounted. Picking up the hot tub victim's book, he tried to decipher her scrawl. The old gal had a lot of appointments, mostly with doctors. Dustin rummaged across his desk for the printouts from the cell phones of the other VICs. He went to the calendars and compared them.

"Interesting. Could he be the perpetrator?" Would this be enough for a warrant? Not likely. For now, he'd conduct an interview to see where this led. Dustin dashed out the door.

The posh reception area held a dozen padded chairs. Six on each side against the walls with end tables, all perfectly lined up across from each other. Dustin counted four magazines in a straight row on each table. Did they use a ruler?

He approached the streak and smudge-free Plexiglas. A petite, fifty-something brunette receptionist pushed a button, and it slid open. Her eyebrows raised, she asked, "May I help you?"

"Yes. I'd like to see Dr. Harper." A vague memory crept in that he might know this man.

"I don't believe I have you on the schedule. Do you have an appointment?"

Dustin showed his badge. "Detective McCall. I have a few questions for Dr. Harper."

"He isn't in today. I can set up an appointment for you."

"Ma'am," He looked for her name. "Sheila, this is in regard to an investigation. Is he at home?"

She shook her head. "He frequents the gym on Monday mornings then takes a drive. The doctor loves driving up 550 and often takes a picnic and a hike. He's a photographer and shoots breathtaking pictures." She pointed to four lined up on the wall behind her—gold aspens. "Of course, he may make his way west or south or even east. Most times, he's out of cell reception."

Dustin looked at the time. Noon. The guy was rambling around in paradise when Dustin needed to ask him about his whereabouts on five occasions. "Thank you." A talkative receptionist was a good thing to remember.

He started to leave then stopped. "Are Mondays his only day out of the office?"

"He has regular patients who rely on him, so he sees patients Tuesday through Friday and every other Saturday. Also, he's out of the office on Thursday afternoons. He is very reliable and punctual. His patients know they can count on him and trust him with all their worries. They love him. You should see him yourself. He has a very good listening ear. You seem stressed. Are you sleeping? He can help you."

He knocked his knuckle on the glass. "Thanks for the sales pitch. I'll keep that in mind. What are his hours?"

"Nine to noon and one to five."

"Sheila, you've been most helpful, but please don't impede my investigation by telling Dr. Harper I'm looking for him." Dustin nodded. On his way to the door, he saw photography awards and official documents for achievement hanging in perfect lines one on top of the other. One framed a patent for some kind of inventive way to developing photographs. Yep, a brainiac.

Hiking to his car, a nagging question pestered him. Why did the doctor take so much time off? One thing he observed, Sheila lit up when she described his attributes. Dr. Harper had a groupie for a receptionist.

He also noticed a neat stack of blue notecards on her desk.

What next? Drive around looking for him? Call his cell? No. He needed to see the good doctor's reactions to his questions.

Chapter 10

The report stated the cause of death—hydrochloric acid. Dustin looked it up. He spoke to the empty room. "Nasty stuff." If it had gone through water, it would've hydrolyzed or lessened in potency. Now he understood the reason for the other canister and the rerouting of the water line to go from the canister to the shower. "The perp would've emptied the shower water line then opened the valve on the canister to send it to the showerhead." That meant he roamed the house. He could've killed him face-to-face or while he slept.

Dustin rubbed his temples. Not enough sleep.

Again, he asked the questions plaguing him. Did the reporter have it right? Too complex for him? Did he need help? After all, how many times had he become so engrossed in his thoughts that he didn't hear someone approach his door? He was losing his edge. His observation. His prowess.

No. He determined not to fall down Alice's wonderland of distorted views. Negative thoughts undermined everything. For years, he'd proven himself and he'd do it again. He'd stand tall, push forward, and solve these murders.

Earlier in his search at the crime scene, he found two bottles of sleeping pills. One for Burt and one for Kim. She confirmed they took them regularly. Dr. Harper prescribed them.

Dustin sent an officer to check the rest of the house and as he thought—no hot water. It had been diverted to the death tank. Any faucet would've been dangerous. The wife said they had hot water the day before and her husband was the only one to shower. So that meant the perp did all his work while the couple slept. "How did he know Burt, and not Kim, would step into the death trap? Did it matter to the perp?"

The ingenious thing the murder added to assure success—the locking mechanisms that kept the shower nozzle from closing and the door from opening. After the hot water faucet was turned on, a piece of metal came out. A matching faucet with the device inside the knob replaced the original one stopping it from turning off. A bolt came out when the shower door closed. Poor Burt had no way of escape. What an agonizing way to die. Dustin's shoulders slumped. "Dear God. Give me something. I've got to catch this sadist."

Waiting for Dr. Harper to arrive home seemed a good idea. Dustin cupped his hand over the watch's face to read the time while blocking the light. The digital numbers showed twelve-forty-seven. Stakeouts were part of the job, although when even he arrived at eleven PM, he thought he'd find Harper home. The SUV's windows open for the cool breeze, he hunkered down in his vehicle up the street with the best view of the house and waited.

Still no sign. He wished he were in an R.V. with access to a toilet and fresh hot coffee, instead of the cold, stale joe he sipped. A bed sounded amazing. He didn't remember the last good night's sleep. When this resulted in an arrest and conviction, he'd take a vacation. Marry Malena if she still wanted him. He'd neglected her but it couldn't be helped.

Earlier, he swung over to the home of Ms. Pérez to take a closer look at her keys. Not surprised, he found they'd been charred and he took pictures to document the scorched marks. Years ago, he learned a blackened key, clear tape, and plastic like a credit card could be used to make a duplicate. The three victims' house keys showed blackened teeth. More proof she wasn't the monster who did these vicious crimes. This also explained why her prints were clear and sharp with nary a smudge underneath. The Good Lord nudged that memory of key copying into the forefront of his brain. Otherwise . . .

Dustin refocused on the bright lights of Harper's house that shone against the dark sky. Most of the houses emitted an abundance of light—a reminder of Durango's high alert. Normally dark neighborhoods now taxed the electric grid. The touristy town sat at the base of the San Juan Mountains. Aviators must view Durango like a diamond against black velvet.

That morning, he researched Doctor Fredrick Harper and realized that over a dozen years ago, when a rookie, he had arrived first on the scene of a truck and motorcycle crash. The brutal wreck left both drivers injured and on the way to the hospital. Right afterward

Dustin got assigned to a search and rescue in the mountains that took almost a week. Then he had taken his scheduled vacation, so he neglected to follow up on the accident.

Sudden headlights momentarily blinded Dustin. A rugged off-road vehicle pulled into Harper's three-car driveway. Dustin drove to park perpendicular behind it. He slipped out and intercepted the doctor. "Dr. Harper, I'm Detective McCall. You're a hard man to track down. I'd like to have a word with you."

"What's this about?" He sneezed.

"Bless you." Dustin said out of habit.

"Do you realize what time it is? Appointments start early tomorrow."

"I'm aware of your office schedule." Dustin noticed the caked mud and dirt and pointed to the immense, rugged tires. "That's a massive four-by-four. Where've you been?"

"Not that it should concern you. But I've been up around Rincon Ridge."

"In the dark?"

"The lights of Durango are impressive. I wanted to shoot it." He pulled open the back door.

Dustin put his hand on his holster. "Whoa. Stop. What are you doing?"

He frowned. "Easy. Retrieving my equipment." He coughed. "I never leave my camera in the truck."

"Nice and slow."

Harper huffed, reached in, and grabbed a large nylon case. "I assume you don't have a warrant to check this but I'll ease your mind." He carried it to the hood, set it down, unzipped the padded compartment, and pulled out a DSLR Cannon. "This isn't a toy. I assure you, I stood—crouched—up there taking shots." He pulled up a few to show Dustin.

"Impressive." Dustin had to admit the man knew photography.

"Can you tell me why you ambushed me in my driveway?"

"Where were you on these dates?" Dustin pointed at a calendar with the five dates circled.

"Off the top of my head, I can't be specific. Ah, the fifth and the twelfth, I took photos up around Baldy and Missionary Ridge."

"Can you prove it? Anyone with you?"

"Birds. A few deer. I captured a fox. Why?"

"Five of your patients were murdered."

Harper's eyes popped open. "Five? What? Who?"

"You didn't realize you were missing the appointments of Colin Raffey, Jane Dixon, Regina Billings. . .

"Oh God!" He put his hand over his face.

Dustin stepped within inches of Harper. His voice grew. "Ted Wilson and Burt Swanson. You remember them." His finger jabbed Harper in the chest. "Let their names burn into your mind." Anger flared and his voice rose to a shout. "Now tell me again. Where were you?"

Soft words came from the man. Instructions to be kept. Another ingenious murder to execute. Every detail had to be adhered to. All about timing. Precision. "That's right. One more quarter turn. Good. Careful. Put the screwdriver into your pouch." Dropping it would be disastrous. "Now, flip the switch to on. Climb down, drive the lift, and park it on the trailer. Leave the way you came. I'll be watching."

On each hand, he rubbed his fingers and thumbs together while he observed his peon doing as told. The flunky slid into his beat-up car and drove off.

The man hated the times when his subordinates were off-camera. He heard their breathing and any other noises around them but couldn't see what they were doing. Music in their vehicles was forbidden. Besides, they had horrendous taste in what they called music.

Another monitor showed the truck towing the lift drive off at a slow speed. "Good job. Take it to its home."

A half-hour later, the first worker crawled into bed and the master said, "Good job. You will fall back to sleep and forget all that transpired. . .uh. . .happened tonight. Sleep well and wake refreshed."

The man almost choked on his words. He hated coddling.

Tori experienced sleep deprivation, yet she didn't remember not sleeping. Maybe she should take sleeping pills. Maybe she wasn't going into REM. Maybe she needed more exercise.

Too tired to exercise, she sprawled on the bed and turned on the television. An ad for a cruise captured her attention. "Oh, I wish. If only I had the money and someone to go with." A sigh trickled out. She had lived with migraines so long, she rarely went anywhere besides work. Not even on a date.

Years ago in seemingly another world, she experienced her last strong relationship. Decades flitted by. Noley had been fun. Adventurous. Then he'd been in a terrible accident and underwent surgeries one after another. Scarred. Rehab. She didn't keep up with him. If he passed her on the street, she'd probably not recognize him from the plastic surgery to reconstruct his face. Oh well. In all likelihood, he healed and found someone better. She shrugged.

Soon after, her migraines started. Occasional ones bumped along for a couple of years then became regular horrific, long-lasting ones. She barely managed to keep her job.

Now migraine free, she could step once again into the dating scene. How should she go about it? Go to a bar? Malena would kill her. No. There were singles at church. She should join that singles class. Yes. That's what she'd do. The singles class would be more fun than the class Malena attended. Yes. Singles. Yes. Next Sunday. Yes. Yes. . .

"Good morning, Durango. The traffic is light so get your morning on. Tourists will start in about an hour."

The voice jarred Tori awake. "Morning?"

A sliver of light around the window shade told her the sun had popped over the mountains. Last night, she must have fallen asleep while watching television. She stretched. Moaned. Her arms hurt. Why? Did she lift weights in her sleep? She found the remote and flipped the morning show off. Time to take a shower. Maybe the hot water would help her sore muscles. On the way to the bathroom, she massaged her biceps and wondered.

Chapter 11

Dustin scanned him from head to toe. Officer Kent stood at the ready, as if for inspection. The man spoke volumes from his confident stare and glistening uniform to his black patrol boots. Did he polish them?

"Kent, you're a good officer. You've handled each of these murder scenes with accuracy and integrity."

"Thank you, sir."

Dustin scratched his unshaven cheek. After three hours of sleep, he showered but didn't shave. "Also, good instincts. Have you thought about stepping into the role of a detective?"

"As a matter of fact, I put in for a transfer last month."

"Did you?" He nodded. "Marlow must be managing the paperwork. It's probably on hold since his surgery. I'd like to fast-track the transfer and assign you as my second. Until it's official, I'd still like to run things by you. A second opinion is helpful."

"Yes, sir. You work better when you have an attentive audience. These four walls don't work as well as you and Detective Marlow did." Half of his mouth lifted in a smirk.

Dustin laughed. "Yeah, I'm well-known for my

verbal eloquence even when alone."

"You could say that, sir."

"As Marlow would say, let's dispense with the 'sir.' Because of heart issues, Marlow had no choice but to expedite his retirement. I'll make a few calls and we'll see if we can get you set up here, even temporarily." Dustin thumbed to the other desk across the room. "Marlow's desk needs an occupant and this room could use a breathing sounding board. I'm sure you fit the criteria." He suppressed a grin and nodded then studied the man. "As you already do, please feel free to say what's on your mind, and also feel free to express any hunches you have." Dustin looked Kent in the eye for a full six beats. "I'll clear off his desk." He rose and shook Kent's hand. "Welcome aboard."

"Thank you, Detective. I'll wait for the orders and step in when possible with huge listening ears." He grinned and swaggered out the door.

Glad for some humor, Dustin went to his partner's desk. He rubbed his hand over the worn wood. Many case files shuffled across this surface. Jim Marlow had seasoned him and became his friend. His family invited Dustin over for barbeques. They watched televised games together. One time when things were quiet in the office, he took Jim up to the high meadow where Dustin loved to ride. Since Jim wasn't used to sitting on top of a horse, Dustin gave Jim a docile mount, which his partner seemed to enjoy.

He missed his mentor. It'd be difficult to see Kent behind this desk which reminded Dustin of his friend—solid and worn in the most dapper of ways.

A clear plastic bag sat on top of the desk containing the blue warning card Jim received and identical to all of the others found at crime scenes. Why had Jim and not he received the card with the warning? Did the perp think he couldn't solve the case?

Stand in line.

He straightened his spine. He'd prove them all wrong.

Clear of personal items, only one photo frame stood in the corner. Dustin picked it up. Jim's family, all gathered last Thanksgiving. Dustin remembered having taken the picture. He'd bring it the next time he went to see how Jim was doing. Phone calls weren't the same, but apparently, Jim gained strength each day and had begun a new diet and exercise routine. The drawer's contents were tidy. He tugged the larger file drawer open and pulled the files, carrying them to an empty chair beside his desk. He'd sort through them later—after this infuriating case was solved.

Tori paced while she spoke to the receptionist on her cell phone. "You have to get me in to see him. Dr. Harper will know what's happening to me. It must be a side effect of the hypnosis. Please."

"As I told you, he's booked solid. I put you on the waiting list, and I'll call you if we have any cancelations. Remember you do have an appointment in two weeks."

The woman's chipper voice grated on Tori, and she clinched her jaw. "Thank you." She tossed her phone onto her bed and followed it to bury her head in the pillows. What was happening to her?

Sleep-deprived early mornings were always difficult. The man moved closer, readying for the action to unfold. He loved this. Born for this. His life's work. All of his masterful achievements, discoveries, and inventions paled in comparison to this. With a twisted curl of his lips, he scanned the rooms of each residence portrayed in black and white in the rows of monitors. He viewed them each, frame by frame—memorizing the occupant's movements and learning their quirks and routines. He took note of where they were vulnerable.

Hours passed but seemed mere moments when a buzzer sounded. Time to watch the next victim. Although a brilliant scheme, she wouldn't suffer like the last one. It made him sad. Too bad.

The man swigged from his ever-present magic bullet. The leer on his face reflected back from the screen when the woman came into the frame.

Daily tuned into her, he already memorized all her movements. "Ready, my dear?"

She crossed to the center of the room where a miniscule wooden table stood in the expansive round entry. "Stand there. Perfect. Now open your mail." A normal person would have taken her mail to her sitting room where she could open, read, and answer. The stacks were impressive. Fan mail. After she slit open and pulled out a few letters, she bent to smell the fresh flowers. Always the flowers. The vase constantly held freshly cut flowers when she came to read the previous day's mail. He didn't understand why she didn't read them the day they came. Her habit made her death easy for him and it would all be caught on instant video. "Yippee!" The world would get to view his masterful work. This should bother the detective.

Fantastic.

The crystal vase held a dramatic display of what he knew to be red and white blossoms with greenery, although he saw it in black and white. The wannabe actress set her phone on an easel positioned to capture her movements on video. He watched her mouth move as she played before the camera. She touched each blossom, as if cupping the chubby cheek of a baby. A few she drew close to catch the fragrance. The woman probably thought the blossoms were made just for her. Well, she hired a gardener to prune, fertilize, and water her precious roses and gardenias inside a hothouse on her estate.

He scoffed, "So they *are* made just for you."

As predicted, her performance in front of the phone camera stalled her at the site in time for the incident.

What's taking it so long? He had calculated every turn of the screw. "It should happen right…"

In a swoosh, the chandelier fell and crashed down upon her. The massive four-hundred-pound obsidian and wrought-iron fixture knocked her into the vase of flowers, which shattered. The table splintered and pancaked her under the light fixture. He couldn't blink for fear he'd miss a twitch.

No movement.

"Bwahaha." The man peered at the TikTok screen and watched the live recording while the cell phone stayed in action. He also made a recording of the

TikTok video to play later over and over again.

He directed the video to replay so he could watch it from the phone's perspective thus the world's. The picture jerked around during the phone falling. The body landed a split second after the phone. Blood splattered the screen. Her wide eyes revealed the young life draining away. "Thank you, my beauty, for sharing your final moments with the world."

Chapter 12

Coming back from the service entrance to the front of Anna Buckingham's house, Dustin reached the entry where Kent stood guard. He opened the door and stopped right inside the threshold to take in the first view of the crime scene. The copper smell hit his nose before the pool of blood drew his attention.

"How in the world?" Dustin observed the scene. "Kent, any ideas? An accident or is this poor young woman a victim of our serial?" He and Kent put booties and gloves on.

"Sir, I think we need to get techs aloft, to look for the cause." Kent pointed to the high ceiling.

Dustin whistled. "Line up scaffolding and such to get them up there. Find a professional lighting expert to consult. After we check the body, we'll have a talk with the cook."

"Oh, lookie here. Not a random kill." Dustin picked his way around the pool of blood to the inevitable blue card stuck to a piece of the chandelier. Kent popped open a plastic bag and Dustin dropped it in.

Dustin squatted next to the fatality. "What's the

lowdown?"

Kent wrote in his notebook as he spoke. "You already know the cook found Anna Buckingham and called 911. The deceased is one of those TikTok influencers." He reached over to her phone and shut the screen down. "The phone didn't turn off. This whole thing could be on video."

Dustin held an open evidence bag. "Good to know. Maybe it caught something useful." He frowned. "Wonder why the perp didn't think of that? Continue."

"Buckingham started her life with money but she amassed exponentially more when she put herself out there and now has an enormous fan base. These must be fan mail." He used his pen to tap a few of the scattered white envelopes and postcards away from the oozing blood.

Dustin used tweezers to pick up the mail closest to the body before they soaked up too much blood, and he dropped them into an evidence bag. "Anna didn't have a chance. The thing must weigh a couple hundred. The shards in her neck made her demise quick. Must've bled out. That's a vast pool."

"Her face shows trauma from smashing onto the table. Broken nose, I think." Kent looked toward the open door. "Here's Walter now."

"Bag the mail and these wires and this piece of…well whatever it used to be." Dustin stood and met the coroner at the door while Walter's assistant headed to the victim. "Sorry about this. I know you're understaffed because of all the deaths. We're not ruling anything out. Intentional? Accident? Give us what you can, when you can. Our team will assist in removing the weapon. We think it used to be a light fixture. The whopper came down from up there." Dustin tilted his head up to view the ceiling.

"We'll do our best. Like you always say, don't rush."

Dustin turned his attention to Walter and nodded. "Yes, time is of the essence, but so is accuracy. I'll stick with accuracy. But hurry it up, all the same." He tightened his lips and patted him on the shoulder.

Walter's assistant pulled the thermometer from the body. "Temp and rigor, best guess, I'd say—" he sighed—"less than an hour. With this much blood, I'm guessing exsanguination."

Dustin figured so. Something on the floor caught his attention. Tracks. Careful not to walk too close, he followed them. The tracks led through a sitting room to an outside door. He opened the door to find a fenced-in patio. Studying the giant pavers, he discovered cracked ones. Those led him to a gate. The unlocked gate led off to the driveway.

Back at the body, he motioned for Kent. "These tracks go out through a patio to the driveway. I think a lift came across this floor to take our killer up there." He pointed to the ceiling. "To the bracket holding the light fixture. After taking pictures, we can use a lift to get up there."

"Good eye. The tracks are barely visible. Much easier for one man. What about the noise of a motor?"

Dustin nodded. "Right. I thought the same. Ready to find answers?"

Now, they would interview the woman, who at least in her mind, ran the place and held to her title as a shield of honor, The Cook. Kent stopped to talk to an officer and swept his hand toward the fragments and mangled pieces, then pointed to where the chandelier should be hanging. Dustin's spine tingled as he thought of the impact on Anna. He prayed death was instantaneous.

"No. You weren't told to ring the bell. Lunatic," the man shouted into the empty room, where no one could hear, not even the target of his wrath. His pulse went crazy. A vein stuck out in the man's neck. The weak link—the one who veered off his instructions. The distinct tone of the doorbell when his puppet ran away gave him apoplexy. Next, he recognized her labored breath and the crash as she vaulted into the bushes near the stream, where he'd earlier told her to hide.

He drummed his fingers on the armrest of his chair. "This better not fall off the rails. Everything is planned to the microscopic detail. Your independence has become a problem. You might need to have an accident. A collision with…What shall it be?" All of his fingers flew in agitation as his mind went through dozens of scenarios. He didn't have time to be furious. The man fisted his hands to quiet them.

He took deep breaths to slow his heart, then turned to the straw that awaited a large swallow of his ever-present drink.

Back in control, he pushed a button and spoke in hushed tones into the microphone. "Dear, you did well. Remove your hoodie but take it with you. Follow the stream to where you left your car. Remember, keep your stereo off while you drive home."

He took another draft of his drink and thought about all the work that had gone into his obsession. One small variant off the design, everything might crumble. He couldn't let that happen. Thinking on her own came with a price. He sneered, "You'll pay, my dear."

On the way to the kitchen, Dustin warned Kent, "Hope you like tea. Drink it even if you don't. The cook is very English, if you know what I mean."

Dustin found the woman where he'd led her earlier, still seated on a chair in the well-equipped kitchen. The first to arrive on the scene, he encountered the distraught woman out in front of the house. He discovered her role in the domestic staff and asked her to take him around the back into the kitchen, where she would feel more comfortable and suggested she make tea.

The plump, older woman sat at the table with a cup of tea in front of her. A white teapot with pink flowers rested on a trivet. Three matching empty cups and saucers, cream and sugar bowls, and dainty spoons, all neatly placed on the table. Good. She had the presence of mind to make tea and lay a table, or did she do it out of habit?

Dustin dipped his head toward the woman. "Mrs. Downey, this is Officer Kent." He pointed to his new partner. "Kent, I'm happy to introduce you to Mrs. Downey, who I'm sure knows all the ins and outs of the household. We have some questions for you, ma'am.

May we enjoy a cup of tea with you?"

She nodded. "I thought you were one to understand the power of tea, and I made plenty. Nice and strong is what my mum used to say. How will you take yours?"

"The way you made yours, I'm sure." He took a seat. Dustin hated it "white" or with milk, but he wanted to loosen the lips of the sweet old English gal.

The cook poured, used a tong to lift a cube of sugar, and added a large splash of milk. Downey handed Dustin the cloudy drink. Oh boy.

"How would you like yours, Officer?"

"Ah, one lump, but no milk today. I'm on duty."

Mrs. Downey lifted her eyebrow and swatted the air. "Oh, you." She giggled. "I'll give you a strong cup." She poured and added the sweetener, then sobered. "That poor girl. As difficult as Miss Buckingham could be, she still didn't deserve to die like…" Downey's voice trailed off and she dabbed her eye with a white hankie she pulled from her ample bosom. His mom used to call that space a high pocket.

Dustin's large hand encompassed the dainty cup. He set his face in stone and gulped. Although on the hot side, it seemed easier to do it in larger but fewer swallows. "Give us a rundown of what Anna does on her normal day. Or an atypical day? Please tell us all you can. You probably know her the best because you prepare her meals. That's an intimate activity."

Mrs. Downey ducked her head and smiled. "Miss Anna liked me. You might say I came with the house. Once Anna tasted my cooking, she wouldn't have it any other way." She splayed her hands. "The last tenants were dears. I hated to see them go. But they were off, back to New Zealand. They begat three adorable children—triplets—easy to pacify those darlings." She sipped her tea.

"Who all works here?" Dustin noted Kent with his pen poised over his notepad.

"The gardener, the housekeeper, and her domestics—it was her day off. A chauffeur, and let's see—," She looked up and frowned, "Me. She determined we didn't need the butler, so he was dispensed of shortly after she arrived."

"When did Anna come to live with you?" Dustin took another jarring swig while he waited for her to speak.

"About eighteen months ago. Yes, after Christmas, during the hard time of the pandemic. That's the other reason I didn't want to be put out."

"Was she easy to work for?" Dustin sat back and crossed his long legs.

"At first all was pleasant, but it appeared Miss Anna experienced some sort of falling off that 'tick' thing on the internet." She wiggled her fingers as if brushing away a fly and took another sip.

Dustin nodded. "TikTok."

"I suppose. Anyway, her fellows didn't support her or some such nonsense."

"So Anna got upset that her *followers* on TikTok were down? They unfollowed her?" Kent scooted his cup closer to her. "I'll take a little more, Mrs. Downey."

The cook grinned and poured. "Yes, I believe that's what Miss Anna said. Stormed around, she did, and demanded flowers replaced each day instead of every three. Next, Miss wanted what she called amazing cakes and pastries. I had my head in the oven more often to make and decorate scrumptious delights, only for my pastries to be photographed or filmed." Downey shrugged. "Shot, as they say, by her phone. Miss never did eat them. On occasion, she'd slide her finger in the icing for a taste. A look of delight would appear on her pretty face, then she'd say, 'throw them out.'" Downey glanced around, then leaned forward. "Instead, I gave them away, to the gardener, postman, even delivery people. I hated throwing them all away."

Her whispered voice drew Dustin and Kent to lean toward her. They were privy to her secret. This didn't help the case but it gave them insight into the victim's frame of mind.

Dustin whispered back, "I agree. Can you tell me if she had appointments with any doctors? Or counselors?"

Downey lifted an eyebrow and wiped her mouth with a napkin. Still, in her conspiratorial tone, she said, "Dr. Harper. He hypnotized her for migraines and weight loss." She nodded.

Dustin kept his voice low. "Ah. Did it help?"

"Anna stopped complaining about her migraines but she's always been a slight figure." Cook shrugged.

He nodded, patted her hand, and raised his voice to normal. "So, Mrs. Downey, tell me what transpired today."

She sat up straight. "It began as a normal day. I made breakfast, eggs Benedict, which she said were beautiful and used her phone every which way. Then she took three bites and went off to open her mail. I just put the dirty dishes in the sink and wiped the table when I heard an awful crash. That's when I ran and found her under that monster." She shook her head. "I knew putting up lava rock on the ceiling would come to no good. What happened to hanging lovely silver and crystal?"

Dustin redirected her to the topic. "Help yourself to more tea. Did Anna always open her mail there at the table?"

The cook poured more of the brew into her cup. "Yes. From those fans."

"Did you see anything strange yesterday? Anyone here that shouldn't be? Anything out of the ordinary?"

Downey shook her head at every question. "Not many visitors came to the house unless she invited her gang of friends over but that happened last week. An exuberant party, for sure."

"Do you have their names?" Dustin held his empty cup close to his chest for fear she'd fill it.

"No, but I'm sure you will find their names in her phone. That thing has everything." She nodded. "Anna told me."

"It's peaceful here." Dustin looked around. "Is it always this quiet?"

"Finally." She shook her head and sighed. "Anna kept music or other such racket going nonstop even during the night. 'Twas piped throughout the house. Usually, I sleep with earplugs. I turned the music off after…" She dabbed her eyes again.

"Thank you very much, Mrs. Downey. You've been most helpful." Dustin patted her forearm. "And the superb tea did its fine work. Has the lava monster of lighting hung there long?"

The cook cocked her head. "I assume the artificer installed it. Tis always been here as long as I have."

Dustin rose and carried his cup and saucer to the sink. "I'm not sure how much longer we will be here.

We'll need to bring in some equipment to check how they installed and hung the light fixture." He went back to the woman who remained seated, cradling her cup. "Here's my card. If you think of anything surrounding today or about Anna, please call me. Do you have a place to stay while we investigate? We can't have you or the rest of the staff going into that part of the house."

Sadness clouded her features. "Not to worry, we will find someplace. We need to band together in these dire circumstances."

"Let us know how we can get in touch with you. There might be more questions."

Mrs. Downey closed her eyes. "Right."

Kent put his dishes in the sink. "Thank you for the tea."

"Yes. You laid a wonderful table, and we thank you for the informative and delightful chat." Dustin briefly bowed over her outstretched hand.

"Toodles." She blushed and wiggled her fingers at them.

Dustin led the way back to the scene. Nothing remained—everything bagged and taken away. The empty room with the mocking dark red stain on the white tile floor showed the bitter reality. He peered up at the high ceiling and shook his head. How did that thing come down? And at that precise moment?

Careful not to disturb the crime scene tape, Dustin pulled the door closed and stomped to the vehicle. Kent went to his car and spoke over its hood to Dustin who already had the door to his SUV open. "What was that about?"

Dustin chuckled as he slapped on his cowboy hat. "Just helping a witness open up. I hoped it would've yielded more but at least we got some caffeine. I'm sure if something comes to mind, she won't hesitate to contact us. And we know our VIC's phone has everything. Let's pray it does."

With the engine running and AC going full blast, Dustin pulled up TikTok to view Anna's videos, turning down the music. He whistled. Yep. That'll get attention. He scrolled to the latest one.

In the video, Anna caressed and smelled her flowers, while "Flowers" by Miley Cyrus played in the background. A distinct crash sounded over the song, and the screen's view went sideways, shook, then stilled landing within inches of her now battered face. Blood splattered the screen and bits of the lava rock and metal settled around her. Her eyes opened in a vacant stare. "What the heck? This'll go viral unless we can get it taken down. The media will crucify me."

The phone kept recording her still body as the song played on. Dustin heard a scream. Other noises were distinct from the music. "That must be Mrs. Downey discovering the body. What a sight." He closed down TikTok and pulled out of the neighborhood.

Dustin's phone rang through his Bluetooth as he drove back to the station. "Hi, honey."

"Dusty. I got a creepy delivery. Can you come?" Malena sounded as if she'd been crying.

"What do you mean by creepy?" He took the next corner to change directions.

"Dead flowers."

Dustin turned the siren on and floored the accelerator. “On my way.”

Chapter 13

The moment Dustin ran up onto the porch, Malena opened the door. He took her in his arms. "Let's go inside and you can tell me everything."

She snuggled against his shoulder. "My doorbell rang and I answered. A flower box sat on the welcome mat. I looked all around the street but didn't see anyone. It held a card. Sorry I touched it. I didn't know it would be…well, anyway, I read it. Here."

Dustin's heart plummeted. He pulled a glove out of his pocket and took the haunting blue card.

I hope you like my flowers.
Once they were alive
Now they're dead
Just like me.
Anna Buckingham
Who's next?

A threat. Toward Malena? Doubtful. Toward him? "Where are the flowers?"

"I got my cleaning gloves before picking them up. They're in the kitchen."

Dustin followed Malena to the counter. A white long narrow box appeared innocent enough. "How do you know the flowers are dead?"

"The cellophane window. They appear to be dead roses. See?"

Dustin leaned over them. Through the plastic, he recognized the dried out regal heads.

Why? "Long-stemmed?"

"I assumed so with the length of the box. Anna Buckingham—Isn't she a TikTok person the press got excited about a few months ago? They made her out to be some sort of celebrity?"

Dustin frowned. "Yes. You seem to know more about her than I do. What do you know?"

"Durango's local news stations went all paparazzi. We discovered a celebrity in our midst and the press wanted the young crowd to watch the news, so they sensationalized her and her movements. Pathetic. Didn't you see some of it?"

Dustin shrugged. "I didn't put two and two together. I didn't recognize her. Did you know her?" Why hadn't he? He was losing his edge.

Malena shook her head. "I never met her and wouldn't know her but for the news."

"How'd she become a sensation? Why did people follow her on TikTok?"

"Anna boasted a green thumb with roses and gardenias and took pictures of herself and the flowers. She wore low-cut tops using her assets to draw viewers. The television crews blacked out parts of her shots."

"Gotcha." Why send flowers to Malena? This targeted too close to home. His frustration mounted.

"Not only did she shine as a gardener but also she baked. She made the cutest little cakes. In an interview, when asked why she hadn't opened a bakery, she gave some lame excuse about permits and equipment. The interviewer said, 'Come on, Anna, what's the holdup? Maybe we can help.' Then she laughed. 'Keep an eye out. For the right price, it might happen.'"

"Interesting. I should have you on the payroll as an informant."

Malena snickered. "You couldn't afford me."

"Now, don't start talking like Anna."

"Oh, Dusty." She sighed, and her eyes watered. "Why did she send me flowers, and why does the card say she's dead?"

Again, he pulled her into an embrace. "Let's sit down." He led her to the sofa. "Those flowers will keep for a moment." He sat and pulled her onto his lap. "Honey, moments before you called, I left her house. We arrived there because of an incident. A large light fixture fell on her."

"Oh, no. Is she—?"

"Mal, I'm afraid so. We're investigating what happened. I'll need to take the flowers, so the lab can go over them."

"Well then, you'll need the footage from my door. I may have the person who left the flowers on video."

"What?" Dustin used his finger under her chin to turn her so they were face-to-face. "You deserve a kiss. When did you install a camera?"

"I'll tell you after the promised kiss."

He grinned and when his lips touched hers, everything else fell away, as he enjoyed a moment of respite.

Too soon, Dustin pulled Malena to her feet and they went to view her computer in the spare room. She sat and prompted the program to play the video from the few minutes before the time her doorbell rang. "I purchased the alarm monitoring system after the break-in at my boutique. I figured I should have a network here as well. I installed them both."

"Smart girl." Dustin sat next to her and watched the image of her front porch and yard. "Nice camera."

"I figured if it captured someone, the image needed to be clear to identify that person."

He huffed. "I wish other surveillance owners felt the same."

"I'm sure you do." She squeezed his knee.

"Malena, there's something." He pointed to the screen. A slight figure, head down, wearing a black hoodie and black pants, crept up with the white box. "Come on. Lift your face." Dustin's leg bounced with anticipation.

The person placed the box on the mat and raised a gloved hand to press the doorbell. In a micro-moment, a ski-masked face appeared, then the figure ran away out of sight.

Malena gasped.

"What's wrong? Recognize him?"

"Her. I hope not. I'll play it again."

"Can you slow it down or freeze it?" Dustin stilled and held his breath, eyes glued to the screen.

"Yeah. The software should do it. I played with it when I first got it. Hope I remember how. Let's see." She typed a few keys and the video started again. At the right moment, she pushed a single key and the video froze. "I can't believe it. It can't be."

Dustin leaned forward to get a better look. "Who? Recognize the eyes?"

"Not the eyes. The watch."

Dustin squinted at the fancy watch with the bright pink band and diamond-bordered face. "I've seen it somewhere."

"It's Tori's."

"Your friend with the visions?"

She nodded and put her hands over her face.

Finally, a break in the case.

"But Dusty, it can't be Tori. It's someone else with the same watch. You'll see. She's my friend. Tori wouldn't hurt me. Anyway, she doesn't work for a delivery service."

Dustin stood and returned to the kitchen to look at the box and card again. He pulled out gloves and used them to keep his DNA off the card. No labels. No imprints. Nothing. Dustin went to his car to retrieve an extra-large bag and put the box and card into it.

"I'll follow up with Tori and see where it leads." He kissed her cheek. "Don't worry, I'll be nice, and later I'll tell you what I can. Keep your doors locked. Why don't you stay at Jalyn's? I'd offer to sleep on the sofa, but I rarely get that opportunity—of sleep, I mean."

She ran a hand down his cheek and took his hand. "You look worn out. Dusty your body and mind—well, really, the world's—function better after rest. Didn't you say you have Officer Kent helping you? Can't you two take turns, so you both get some sleep?"

"We're fine." He kissed her again. "The sun is shining and it's a magnificent day in Durango. I'll be okay." Sure I am. Now I'm lying to her?

The walk to the car didn't help. Driving off, the conversation continued, "Who am I kidding? I'm running on recirculated exhaustion."

Chapter 14

"We removed the video from social media."

"Thanks, Kent. One less thing to worry about." On the computer screen, Dustin read the reports on Anna Buckingham. Death from blunt force trauma and exsanguination from the light fixture.

One instrument killed her twice.

Kent sat at Marlow's old desk and studied the same report on his computer.

The pictures his team took showed tool marks on the bracket attached to the fixture's remains. Another picture showed the debris of what appeared to be an explosive device. One set displayed scrape marks on the tile floor where something heavy rolled across. He'd already called equipment rentals in the area. Coming up empty, he now broadened his search west to Cortez, east to Pagosa Springs, and south into Farmington, New Mexico. The north held mountains dotted with refurbished mining towns whose main revenue came from tourists.

Surprising how many places rented one-man lifts extending twenty feet and higher. The average weight hovered around a thousand pounds. Some only six hundred. These small lifts maneuvered up ramps into trailers or pickups for easy transport. Designed narrow enough to fit through standard doorframes. So far, all the rental agreements were to bona fide job sites.

Dustin snapped his fingers. “Purchased. He could’ve purchased instead of renting.”

After a half-hour of calls, he came up with a few names. “Interesting. Our doctor friend bought a lift last month.”

Kent barked a snicker. “Can’t be coincidence. Want me to come with you?”

Harper’s schedule blurred in Dustin’s sleep depraved mind. He checked his watch, calculating. “The Doc will have to wait. First light provides a better time to catch him before he leaves for unsubstantiated parts unknown.” He leaned back in his chair. “Kent, did you know one lone man could easily pull off this murder by using a lift and loosening the screws, then setting a small charge on a timer to explode at the exact time the target stood under the chandelier?”

Kent whistled. “Precise.”

Dustin stood and added Anna’s picture to the growing mural of victims. He ran a finger over the face. “I told Malena I didn’t recognize her.” How could he? She’d been unrecognizable when he saw her. A monster killed her and ripped away her facial identity. Fingerprints, dental records, and DNA needed to prove it. Based on height, weight, hair and skin color, and what the video showed, they were most certain Anna lay in the morgue.

Kent put his phone down. “I found another prominent citizen of our great city who purchased a man lift.”

Dustin cocked his head and sat. “Who?”

"Some professor. Name of Olson."

"Wait a minute. I have him on a list." Dustin picked through screens he opened on his computer. "Yes. Here. I put him on the brainiac list. He's on staff at—"

"Fort Lewis," they said at the same time.

"I can't wait to question him." Dustin rubbed his hands together. "Anyone else smart enough to do this and own a lift?"

Kent shrugged. "Not finding anyone. I'll keep looking and calling those on the list to see if they have access to one."

"Perfect. Get on it." Dustin leaned back in his chair, laced his fingers behind his head, and faced the picture board. "A pretty girl. Did you watch her videos or know about her before?"

Kent nodded. "I looked her up because of the buzz around town."

"I should pay closer attention to those things. I feel old."

Dustin drove his SUV up the professor's winding driveway.

The hairs on the back of his neck stuck out. He sensed someone watched him along the half-mile trek.

Edgy. Leery. Mistrustful. Bullseye—all of those described Dustin. He needed to loosen up in order to obtain answers. Or did that make him a better detective?

Acute Spidey senses?

Dustin focused on what he knew. Professor George Olson was the name Kent found who purchased a lift. Why would a guy who taught theoretical physics need one?

He whistled when the house came into view. A castle with turrets. Why not a moat and a drawbridge? In contrast, the concrete continued to a circular drive with extra parking to the side by the garages. Four bays. He chuckled with anticipation of meeting this guy.

Dustin went to the door and pushed the button under what he knew to be a camera. It chimed eerily like a church bell. He surveyed the area and zeroed in on six more cameras positioned around the drive and closer ones, all facing the door.

Paranoid bugger.

Dustin's perceptions of watching eyes were correct as he drove up the drive. Not imagined at all. Again, the Spidey senses stood at full alert.

A thirty-something man opened the door. Slight build. Short sandy hair. Long-sleeved gray polo buttoned to the top and jeans. Squeaking white tennis shoes. Must not go out much.

"Good afternoon, I'm looking for Professor Olson."

The man nodded.

"Is he here?"

A nod. "In a m-minute. Put this on. S-stay there." He handed Dustin a COVID mask and closed the door.

Strange interaction. The man seemed odd. Lower IQ? Inferiority complex? Stuttered because of nerves?

Mask-wearing regulations ceased a while ago. The younger man didn't wear one so that ruled out germophobe. Fear of strangers?

Dustin checked his watch and shifted his weight. He stared at the doorbell cam. Yep, under surveillance. Grinning, he turned so his host saw the holstered Glock 22. Then he masked up.

In a few moments, the door whisked opened by itself. An empty entry waited. He accepted the invitation. The door clanged shut behind him and bolted, making him jump. Not funny.

Noise came from the next room. Dustin turned. A motorized wheelchair, carrying a scrawny, pale man sailed in, with a swish noise like an old-fashioned lady's' silk dress, to stop a few feet in front of him. Padded brackets held his bald head in place. Straps secured his arms onto the armrest leaving only his hands free to maneuver a joystick. "Good afternoon. You're looking for me? I'm George Olson. Sorry I can't shake your hand. You are?"

"I'm sorry."

"Don't be."

Yikes. "I mean, I should've told the other man. My name is Detective McCall. I have a few questions for you, Professor."

"What can I help you with?"

"Did you purchase a man lift last November?"

"Yes. Why? Do I need a license to operate it?"

Dustin chuckled. "No, sir. Would you humor me and let me see it?"

"Of course. Follow me." The wheelchair turned and proceeded down a hall. Dustin trailed behind, taking in everything. The wheelchair moved at a good clip down the wide marble-floored corridor. They passed a vast kitchen with a suspended counter along one wall, designed, Dustin presumed, so the professor could sit at it and work. Did his arms move? At one end of the room sat an oven and a low shelf held a microwave. The perpendicular side held a counter atop lower cabinets. No upper cabinets. Dustin poked his head in to see a large island with a sink and dishwasher. Functional. Pristine. No personal touches or décor.

They came to a door that opened to four garage bays. The wheelchair whizzed across the low threshold. The polished concrete floor sported a mirror finish and everything appeared spotless and orderly. In the first bay sat a dark blue wheelchair accessible minivan. A souped-up Kawasaki motorcycle occupied the second. No oil leaks.

"That's a nice ride."

"Thank you. I can't bear to get rid of it even though I can't use it anymore. I have Lewis turn it on and rev it for me so I can at least listen to it. Running it every once in a while helps keep it from freezing up inside. I let him roll it to preserve the tires."

Let him?

The next bay held a F250 pickup, but the object of his investigation resided in the last section of the garage. Dustin approached it. "Do you mind if I take pictures?"

"Why? I only use it to lift me to the roof, where I have an observation deck so I can see the stars. I also use it to take me upstairs if I've a mind to do so. My brother is a fair driver of the lift."

"Is Lewis your brother? The one who answered the door?"

"Yes. This baby makes my life a little more pleasant. The door there affords me access to those places. I don't like to use it indoors. It's heavy, around six hundred pounds and it could crack my tile. I would hate that. Come, I'll show you around back."

Dustin followed, frustrated he couldn't take pictures. They went through a door leading to a glass enclosure with a wooden boardwalk-like path circling to the back of the house. At first, the walkway hugged the house on one side of a ravine with a mountain slope on the other. As they traversed, both hills abruptly sloped away and they faced the majestic view of the valley. The glass enclosure kept one from falling off the steep slope. The incredible view spanned from the edge of Durango to the mountains where Silverton nestled. "Amazing view, Professor."

"Thank you." He stopped his motorized chair. "This is the place where the lift takes me above." His long-nailed finger shot up. Dustin peered through a hole in the ceiling to the hallway of the second story. "The bedrooms are up there."

While Dustin watched, a window slid back into place closing the hallway off from the upstairs rooms. Dustin looked closer at the controls on the wheelchair. Another joystick and buttons on the left side. That hand seemed more mobile.

The professor drove farther along. This time Dustin anticipated the window opening. With a slight sound, it slid back. "My observation deck with a telescope is up there." His finger again pointed.

Dustin observed a flat roof, chairs, and the eyepiece end of a telescope. "Wow. Impressive. Did you design your home?"

"How astute of you. Yes. I enjoy design and practicality—form and function. They melded perfectly here. I'm sorry but I'm tired." He turned around in a tight semicircle to lead back through the garage and down the indoor hallway toward the front door.

Dustin stopped at a smooth metal door. “Elevator? Why not use the elevator instead of a lift?”

“That goes down. I teach my classes via broadcast from the basement office. It’s cool and quiet down there.”

“I see.” No buttons operated the elevator. A flat box the size of his hand mounted at hip height appeared to be a handprint reader. Why?

Soon they were at the open front door. “I hope I answered all your questions, Detective.”

Dustin studied the professor’s smug expression. “I may visit again. You’re an interesting man.”

Dustin entered his office and filled Kent in on his encounter with the professor. “The guy is interesting but something bugs me. Highly intelligent. Weird brother named Lewis. We need a background check on both of them. Did you get anything out of Anna’s gardener and other staff?” He sat in his office chair and scanned the victim board.

“The gardener said someone broke into the shed three weeks ago. Some of the best roses were cut and removed but nothing else was missing. I dusted for prints but came up empty.”

Dustin swiveled to face Kent. “Figures. The maniac is immaculate, if nothing else. Never leaves a hair, fiber, or print. He must wear a head covering and shave his body. We need to follow up on the shrink. His patients keep dying."

"I've got that on my notes. Want me to handle it?"

"Nah, I'll shuffle him into a corner if I can find him. Early tomorrow before he leaves, I'll park behind him and get him to talk about her and the lift he acquired. If he isn't cooperative, I'll pull him in for questioning."

Kent nodded. "We need a name for our killer besides all the adjectives that fit."

"Yep and we don't want the media to get wind of the blue calling card. Hm. I like the word you used earlier—precise." Dustin snapped his fingers. "The Precision Murders."

"Fits."

Dustin stood. "I held her long enough. Let's go talk to our vision princess."

Tori paced. Her fingers shook. The nerve of them holding her without a reason other than, "We have more questions. Sit tight. We'll be back." Why this room and in this way? She'd be happy to answer their questions, especially from that cute Officer Kent. What else could she tell them? She willingly told them about her visions. Anyway, Malena's boyfriend didn't believe her, so why bring her to the station and leave her in this cold, intimidating room?

The door opened. Startled, she spun around to see Detective McCall and cutie pie Kent.

"Victoria Miller. You remember Officer Kent. We have a few questions for you. Please." He motioned to a cold hard chair, which he pulled out for her. "Have a seat."

She couldn't very well refuse. At least she didn't think so. Sitting, she waited. McCall went around the table and took the chair next to the fine Officer Kent. His kind eyes drew her. What was his first name?

McCall put a folder on the table and leaned back in his chair. "Do you know Anna Buckingham?"

She tensed and straightened. "Who?" They weren't asking about a building but a person this time.

"Anna Buckingham, the TikTok star who lives here in Durango."

Tori shook her head. "I don't do TikTok." Her pulse raced.

Kent shifted in his chair. "The videos showed up on Instagram and Facebook. Anna enjoyed filming her flowers and cakes. You probably saw them."

"I don't do those either. Well, I have a Facebook profile, but I'm never on it." She crossed her arms over her tightening chest. "So, I don't know who you're referring to. Anyway, I see houses. Not people. Why do you ask?"

McCall pulled a picture from the file and slid it in front of her. "Did you envision this house?"

The photo showed a house on the hill like those she dreamed of living in. Huge gray brick with wings, large sparkling windows, and a tile roof. A Cinderella-type house. "No, but I wish I could take a tour."

McCall put another picture in front of her. "Have you seen this building?"

"Isn't that a nursery or hot house?"

"Very good. Have you been there before?"

"I don't think so." As the words came out of her

mouth, heat radiated from within and her breathing quickened.

"But you may have?" McCall insisted.

"Maybe driven by it?" Tori shrugged, took a deep breath, and uncrossed her arms. Relax.

"It's a small-scale hothouse that grows roses and gardenias." McCall's voice grew louder. "If you drove past it, as you suggested, then you were on Anna Buckingham's property. Yet you say you don't recognize her home."

She swallowed. "Oh, well, in that case, I must be mistaken."

McCall leaned forward. "How convenient. You need to be truthful, Ms. Miller."

"I…uh…I don't think I've been there. I'm trying to be helpful." Her pulse pounded in her ears.

McCall kept at her. "Some of the buildings you've envisioned are now the ones you might have driven by? Are you trying to be evasive?"

Tori looked up at the silent Officer Kent, wishing she could pull him to her side. "I'm trying to be helpful like I've been all along."

McCall slid another picture to her. "How about this?"

When she leaned over to get a better look, her heart almost stopped. Hands shaking she moved it closer. "Yes. Yeah. It's kind of blurry but I see it."

McCall pulled the picture away and slapped down a pad of paper and a pencil.

She jerked.

"Draw what your mind's eye shows you."

"Okay. You don't have to be mean. Just ask."

"Would you like some coffee or water?" Officer

Kent leaned over and rested his hand on her forearm.

Tori beamed into his kind eyes. Needing a distraction, she said, "Yes. Coffee. Black, please." Tori straightened the pad and lifted the pencil. Her left hand flew across the page, creating the image she briefly saw. Just like her visions. At first, they were blurry, then they became crystal clear as she drew. Engrossed in her sketch, the room faded away. An artist at heart, she enjoyed drawing with her favorite medium, the pencil. This one paled to the ones she preferred but it worked fine.

A hand holding a cup lowered it next to her. She jolted, almost knocking it over.

"Easy there." Kent steadied the cup.

"Thank you." After a grateful sip, she focused her attention on the drawing and shaded a few more places. Satisfied, she swiveled it toward the men.

"You're an artist. This picture is better than the one we showed you. Let's do a comparison." McCall turned the photo over and put it side by side with her drawing and shifted them to face her. "You added more detail. Amazing, yours looks exactly like this one." He plucked another picture from the folder and set it down next to her. "See, you added shrubs and the basement window like this original. Also, you enhanced the figure's clothing. You must know the person, or you *are* the person."

Chapter 15

Dustin watched the color drain from her face.

Tori gasped. “No! This can’t be.”

“You were there. Just like you were here.” He slapped down the photo of the figure with the watch on the right hand ringing Malena’s doorbell.

She gasped again.

Dustin jabbed his finger at the watch in the photo. “This watch is the same as the one you’re wearing on your right arm.”

Her left hand covered the watch and held it tight to her chest. A rapid shake of her head denied everything. “No. Not me. S-some kind of joke. Can’t be me. I wasn’t there. I didn’t ring a doorbell.” Tori’s hands flew to her face. “Oh, God, it can’t be me. Help me. Please help me.” Racking sobs shook her shoulders.

Kent moved forward. Dustin raised his hand to still him and shook his head. He couldn’t let too much good cop into the equation.

The man spoke aloud to himself. “Not doing so

well in the interrogation, my dear. You've caused me a lot of grief. It's in your best interest that McCall has you in his sights. Maybe they will throw you in jail and toss away the key. Better there than what I planned for you."

He crackled.

Wheezed.

Sipped from his jug.

"Now, I'll need to find a replacement for you." He scanned his list of workers. "Ah, yes, Steven gets promoted. He's attentive to instruction and obedient to a fault. Now we will see if he is what you all need to be, more forgetful and less talkative. Yes. An improvement to you, my lovely redhead.

"They don't have enough evidence to book you, so you should be able to breathe fresh air soon." He scanned the ceiling in the cold room as he pondered his next move.

"Oh, I know what I'll do. Yes." Excitement coursed through his veins. "I'm going to put you on one last assignment. Yes, one more. A tricky one. Do well, and I'll let you walk away from all the fun we've enjoyed. If they zero in on you again and arrest you, or you remember more and blab, then my beauty, it'll be car meets train."

He knew it'd be cutting it close. The plan could only happen if everything else fell into place. Would she follow her routine? He couldn't use her if she didn't.

The man turned his focus on the screens before him where at each address, unsuspecting people went about their lives.

Later he glanced at the time—only a few hours

until the umbra when people were in deep sleep and the action started. Then fun began. An ominous sneer stretched across his tight features.

They didn't have enough to hold her. Dustin dismissed the suspect and directed Kent to walk Victoria out, then stalked to his office and ground out the paperwork on the interview.

After a while, Kent came in and went to work at his desk, giving Dustin a wide berth.

Computer keys clicked away, and Dustin assumed Kent put his observations into the file. At each tap on the keyboard, Dustin's anger ebbed, replaced by weariness. Fatigue caused him to work slower than a sloth in a tree. His eyes burned. The words in front of him blurred. He needed to get some shuteye.

Kent's normal upbeat and talkative temperament contrasted to the overbearing silence in the room. The only sound came from Kent's fingers flying across the keys. Dustin's partner now clenched his jaw.

"All right, what's annoying you?"

Kent's hands stilled. He typed a moment then closed his computer. "Sir, why were you so hard on Victoria?"

Ah. Figures. After all, he liked her. "She lied about not seeing Anna on social media. You discovered she used emojis and commented on a few of her videos."

He blew out a breath and eyed Kent. He needed to help him understand. "My first year as a rookie, I helped question a guy. We played it light. The dude lied to us into believing his innocence. The crook skipped with a bundle of stolen goods. I learned my lesson. Even if the suspect is a friend of someone you love, you can't let your relationships or feelings take over. Truth has to win out. The best way is sometimes harsh."

"Could there be another reason?"

Dustin stood. "I'm going to get food and sleep." He turned on his heel and left the building.

The trees in the landscape of the parking lot danced and shimmered against the denim sky. A gust of wind rounded the corner and barreled into him, knocking him off balance. Dustin picked up the pace to his car to avoid the approaching storm. He put his phone on vibrate instead of the ring tone so he wouldn't hear Malena's call. Tori would complain to Malena about him being a brute.

Dustin shook his head. No choice.

Neither woman would understand he had no other way to get straight answers. He sighed. He couldn't let the only slice of evidence slide away.

Dustin scrubbed his hand over his face. Too many deaths. A killer or a team of killers terrorized the people of Durango. Tori didn't have the wherewithal to orchestrate it but she was involved, and he determined to find out how.

Two major suspects and not enough proof. The doc couldn't produce an alibi for most of the times people died. He was always by himself. Alone at home. Alone in the wilderness. Alone with his patients. What went on in that room where his patients poured out their hearts? A list of deceased patients didn't warrant an arrest. Dustin felt the angst. Not enough on Doctor Harper to bring him in. A guy in a wheelchair couldn't pull them off either.

Weariness washed over Dustin, and depression threatened.

Dark clouds brewed in the western sky. The smell of a storm filled the air. Paper and leaves scattered in front of the unseen force. He tightened his grip on the steering wheel. Summer storms could be harsh and unpredictable, like the case. The unidentified monster created chaos in the lives of the families and the town. No closer to unmasking the devil, Dustin drifted like the paper and leaves scattered with no direction.

A seasoned detective? He snorted. Years didn't automatically make one.

He always loved to solve puzzles. Now, he couldn't even find the missing pieces to the puzzle.

At home, he slumped down on the sofa, ate his tasteless burger from the drive-thru, and drank tepid water. He needed to lay off caffeine in order to get some sleep. He tossed the wrapper in the trash can, checked the hot water tank in the garage, and went for a hot shower. Before stepping in, he turned on the water and looked for locking mechanisms, keeping the door open a crack.

Tonight the man gave orders to multiple players. It was hectic with such short notice, but it had to be tonight, so he pushed his workers harder than normal.

The monitor showed his worker slip into the room and put knockout drops in the target's drink then hide before the target reappeared. When timing came down to the wire, the man got excited and held his breath. He exhaled and congratulated himself with a swig of his drink.

In bed, Dustin turned on the television. The newscaster grated on his nerves with the lighthearted retelling of events. Then the camera panned to one man in a light blue suit who pricked Dustin's attention.

"Now for an update on the murders . . . Crickets, folks . . . Do you hear them? Crickets. Dustin McCall, our town's new lead detective, is obviously in need of help. Our sources tell us a few women were brought in for questioning but there are still no arrests. A killer slaughtered six upstanding citizens in their *own* homes. What does the cowboy do? Nothing."

The newscaster leaned forward on his elbows. "People, get out of Durango.

"Go on vacation.

"Stay out of your homes until the Precision murdering maniac is taken down." A commercial for a rental place came on. Dustin switched off the TV, feeling depressed and extremely sleepy.

The cell phone chirped and Malena answered. "Hey."

"Your boyfriend brought me in for questioning. I can't believe it. What do you see in that man? He's cruel."

Malena clasped the phone tighter as she bore the brunt of Tori's rampage. "Tori, he's doing his job. He must have a reason. I can't speak for him and I didn't see or hear it. I concede he can be intense when he's on the job and there's a murderer on the loose. Look at it this way, my sweet friend, you aren't locked up, so be thankful for that."

Her friend's sigh slapped against the earpiece. "I suppose. It's weird that I could draw the picture almost identical to the real one. I guess he must have reasons."

"Exactly. Tori, pray about it. All this will become clear. I'm praying for you and for Dustin to find the murderer. You want the killings to stop, I'm sure, so your cooperation is vital. You're helping."

"Maybe."

"Sweetie, it's late. You'll feel better after a good night's sleep." Malena managed to calm Tori then phoned Dustin to get his perspective but after ten rings, it went to voicemail.

The storm raged outside, rattling the windows. She cuddled under blankets and worked her feelings into a prayer for Dustin and Tori. Dusty agonized over these killings. Who wouldn't? The case turned nasty when it pulled Malena into the mystery and made her a piece of the puzzle. And Tori appeared to be involved, no matter what she declared, and Malena found evidence to that fact in a non-biased video. Could they all be wrong about Tori's involvement? Prayers went heavenward on Tori's behalf and pleaded with God that Dustin solve the case before someone else got hurt or worse.

After a half hour of intercessory prayer, she clicked on the TV and her lament increased when the newscaster defamed her sweetheart.

"How could he?" Dustin was an amazing detective. He helped save countless lives over the time she knew him. He not only investigated and solved murders, he also mounted his horse to track people lost in the mountains. Why did the newsman defame her fiancé and incite panic?

The man watched until his entire crew ascended onto the property of the unsuspecting target.

One by one, they entered. Multiple trips. Back and forth.

Giddiness swept through the man. Each reptile deposited excited him more than the last. He whispered into the electronic-filled room to his minions, "Good job. Yes. Wonderful. Now, slowly depart. Perfect."

Yes. They all did their part and the victim didn't realize the peril. On his way out, his key worker switched the AC to heat in the house.

Merriment quivered through him as the deed went by without a hitch.

Now to wait while sipping his drink. It was so worth enduring a long night.

To one particular participant he directed, "Don't forget the last part before heading to your car and don't let her see you." His eyes focused back on the screen. Thirty-nine slithering beauties should do it. He congratulated himself with a long draw on his drink for pulling it all off on such short notice. Without blinking, he watched, not wanting to miss the next show filled with deadly terror. A crackle left his drooling lips.

Chapter 16

Bang! Dustin woke. A dream? Someone at the window? He replayed the sound in his foggy brain. The storm? Something blocked his view of the clock. Dustin tried to move.

Unable.

Tied up?

Must wake up. The pain from biting his tongue determined his conscious state.

Angling his head to change his view, the built-in nightlights in the hall and bedroom cast enough light for him to discern forms. Snakes. Dozens of them. His heart rate shot to the sky.

He bit his tongue again. Ouch. Not a dream.

How?

The pressure in his chest felt ready to explode like a shaken can of soda—crack the tab and run. Perspiration bathed him.

Hyperventilating.

Pinned.

His mind whirled as he took inventory of the situation.

Breathing too fast.

Movement might anger a snake and he didn't want

to be bitten. His arms and legs, trapped under the blanket and reptiles.

The earlier foreboding of trouble came alive right here in his bedroom.

Should he do one quick move and fling himself off the bed? No. A sideways glance showed reptiles slithered on the floor. He'd never make it out of the room.

Quick, shallow breaths, he willed into slow deeper ones. All about survival.

Snakes—his worst nightmare. Dustin's mind flashed back to when, as a boy, he roamed the range atop his mare, Luna. Wanting to play in the creek, he reined her in to graze. As he dismounted, a rattler startled Luna. She reared. Dustin sailed off, landing on his arm. It cracked. He cried out. The rattler struck the mare, causing her to bolt. Tears clouded his vision. No one heard him in the middle of nowhere—alone and isolated.

He managed to get to his feet. The coiled snake rattled three fat rattles. Inch by inch, Dustin backed away.

Far from the monster, he crafted his t-shirt into a sling. Leaving it on but tugging his good arm out of the sleeve, he used his lucky pocketknife to cut a slit and pull the end through, then secured it by weaving a twig over the opening.

On foot, he searched for his beloved horse, all the while keeping an eye out for more snakes. The useless arm made it impossible to use his fingers to make a shrill whistle. The other hand didn't work quite right to produce a proper strident to bring Luna to his side. Frustration and pain mingled. Tears ran down his face.

Wiping at them with his good arm, he sniffled.

Miserable, he rambled home.

Late for supper, he thought he'd get into trouble. Instead, his mom almost killed him in a bear hug. That's when she realized her boy's temperature soared.

A few days later, Dustin's dad found Luna. The vet said she died from the venom causing swelling that choked off her airway and led to cardiac arrest. From that moment, he possessed a phobia of the slithering monsters. Had he been in the Garden of Eden, he wouldn't have stopped to talk with the serpent as Eve did.

Now, a grown man, the terror of snakes still sliced as deep and recurring dreams often woke him in a sweat. Tonight was no different. Dustin knew they would strike if provoked or frightened.

He always slept on his back propped up on pillows, which right now gave him a good view around the room. How did they get into his bedroom? Did the contractor build his house on a snake pit? No. It hadn't happened before now. There were too many varieties. From the glow from the nightlights, he recognized rattlesnakes, diamondbacks, and the distinctive corals. Also, he thought there might be solid black and plain green. Some he thought weren't poisonous. Not an expert, he didn't know. Cotton mouth on the bed? That species finished off the victim at the second murder. Coincidence?

Every time a serpent moved, his heart skipped. He kept his breath slow for fear of disturbing them. Would he die?

The dark cloud of helplessness started to swallow him. I can't even protect myself—how can I protect the community?

Heart pounding, hot and sticky, frightened, exhausted, and bewildered, he found it hard to think. But he could pray.

At dawn, he watched the light filter through the blinds. The mocking night couldn't end fast enough. His eyes burned from keeping them open. How long would it be before someone missed him and came looking?

In the still of the night, when everyone slept, anticipation filled the man as he watched Dustin wake. His victim's eyes grew enormous. He could almost see the sweat glistening on McCall's forehead. Trapped, the detective barely moved.

The man laughed.

He glanced at the clock and calculated the snakes were sure to come out of brumation becoming more active. Before tonight, the man kept these babies in a cool environment to put them into brumation for transportation purposes. He didn't want most of his workers subjected to snake bites. Enamored with them, he'd amassed a small army of serpents for such a time.

The snakes heated up and began to move. The man's attention riveted as they uncoiled and swerved in slow motion. "So hypnotizing." He chuckled at his own joke.

Snakes slithered. One hungry viper took its time eating another. Impressed, the man cheered it on.

The cameras caught the awake, yet still body of

McCall and the wiggling serpents.

A slow-moving movie. He grinned.

As hours ticked by, his glee morphed into frustration.

Frustration mounted to anger. Sweating, the man convulsed with rage. No snake strike. No apparent heart attack. Not enough terror to kill him? Outmaneuvered, he yelled, "Die. Die. Why aren't you dead?"

The brilliant plan malfunctioned. Backfired. The man's heart pounded at an alarming rate. His neck muscles tightened and veins stuck out. Even the elixir didn't calm him. How to kill McCall? "Think. Think." His fists slammed down.

All through the nocturnal plight, Dustin thought he'd die. Doubts of his worthiness as a detective and future husband cascaded into his soul. The murderer should be behind bars. On his watch, every forty-eight hours, a person died an unimaginable death. Dustin blamed himself for not catching the madman. He'd sworn allegiance to justice. Failing miserably he'd let the town down. The families down. Himself. And most important, his God.

In the quiet solitude with snakes all over him, he had time to pray. Really pray. At first, he pled for a miraculous delivery from the snakes. He reminded the Lord how he led the Israelites out of Egypt, delivered Daniel from becoming lion food, and kept the three friends from burning alive in the fiery furnace. The Lord could rescue him from these slithering monsters. Then his prayers went to asking the Lord to keep him alive. Yearning to marry Malena, he took time to reflect on their relationship and where he needed to step it up. Did he take her for granted? Had he stopped wooing her?

The case consumed him. In desperation, Dustin craved to catch the Precision Murderer and to see Lady Justice get hers. Desiring answers, he prayed for the wisdom God bestowed on Solomon, so he could catch the diabolical killer. His mind muddled and needing assurance, he asked God to show him if he was the right one for the job. Could he—would he—solve the murders? He repeated his whispered prayer, "I'll step down if You want, but if this is my calling, lead me to the monster before anyone else is murdered."

Then he prayed for each person in his life.

Chapter 17

Malena left three messages on Dustin's phone. After no response from him, she climbed in her car, and using Bluetooth, called Kent. "Officer Kent, this is Malena Campbell. I'm trying to reach Dustin but he's not answering. Have you seen him this morning?"

"He's not here. Maybe he's following a hunch. Or visiting Marlow. Last night, he said he went to get food and sleep. He needed both, I tell ya." The officer chuckled.

"Thanks. I'm sure he did. Please ask him to call me when he gets in."

"You got it."

Malena ended the call and drove to Dustin's. Maybe he worked from home. She wished to question—no, beseech him. Atypical of him not to call her back, her worry meter rose. At a stoplight, she drummed her fingers against the wheel impatient for her turn to go. "Come on. Change."

Alarm bells went off in her gut. Something was wrong. What could it be?

The light turned green. Hurry. She slammed her foot on the gas as concern mounted. "Settle down. You can't help him if you get in an accident." She eased off the pedal.

Malena turned onto his street and saw the SUV in the driveway. Relief washed over her. She parked and the pent-up tension seeped from her like water from a melting ice cube. Maybe he decided to work from home. To top it off, she knew he staved off sleep with caffeine. Perhaps he fell into a deep sleep and overslept. The last time she saw him, his bloodshot eyes told the story of his lack of rest. Stress etched lines on his handsome face.

Why did he stay home with a murderer to catch? Not like him. What if sickness overcame him or he had collapsed? She frowned, zipped to the front door, and rang the doorbell.

Waited.

Knocked. "Dusty, it's me. Please open the door."

Waited.

In the shower? Too sick to answer?

Hurrying to the garage, she used the code. The double garage door lifted. Inside she hustled past his personal vehicle almost identical to the official-issued one, except for the lights and radio. Malena knocked then stepped into a dim, quiet house, peaceful as a sleeping baby. "Dusty, it's me."

"Back here." His low voice sounded strained.

Heart pounding, she rushed toward the bedroom. "Are you all right?

"No. Don't come back here. Call Kent and Animal Control."

Already down the hall, she poked her head into the darkened room. "Dusty?"

"Stop!"

The bed seemed alive.

Her eyes adjusted to the dim light.

A scream rose. She clamped her hand over her mouth, swallowing the scream.

Snakes covered him and the bed. Some on the floor. It appeared to her there were hundreds of snakes. All sizes. Wriggling devils filled his room. A few feet away, a rattler reared and hissed at another one.

Tugging her phone to her ear, her quaking fingers didn't work. She whispered, "Call Officer Kent." The cell lit up, ringing. At his answer, her voice trembled. "Kent! Snakes all over Dustin's room." She gasped. "Call animal control. Get here fast. There are diamonds and other kinds. I remember, red touching yellow will kill a fellow. Oh, Lord, Dustin will need paramedics, too. I can't believe this. Too many to count. They slither. Get rescue and the National Guard." She ended the call and looked around her feet then up on the highboy next to her shoulder. Clear. She took a shaky breath. "Dustin, they're on their way. Are you bitten?" She couldn't help the quiver in her voice. Although she knew better, she experienced the sensation of them slithering over her.

He choked out. "Not yet. Can't breathe."

Malena tugged on her shirt that stuck to her body. "It's really warm in here. Did your AC quit?"

"I'm sweating. Nerves? Don't know."

She wanted to run and toss snakes off him. Instead, she scanned all around herself. Still clear. Torn between staying with him and running from the horde of reptiles, her tense body shook. Love won out.

As he waited to be released from bondage, Dustin replayed the last few moments when Malena showed up. He remembered the doorbell startled him and took him out of his mental anguish. Banging on the door caused him to silently beg the person to break in.

The sweetest voice in the world came from near his garage door. "Dusty, it's me."

Relieved, he almost forgot to warn her of the danger.

At the door of his room, Malena took over. His hero.

Pride swelled in his tight chest. This woman, his bride-to-be, spoke like a sergeant into the cell phone demanding a rescue. Shaking hands and a slight quiver in her voice were the only outward signs of the fright underneath her demeanor.

He kept Malena in view, as she soldiered through the ordeal with him. His love for her bounded to heights he never knew possible. She loved him enough to brave this deadly game. Using her phone, she kept in contact to direct Kent and the gang to him.

Not soon enough the rescuers appeared. Thank You, Lord. He'd be free in a while.

Snake handlers and veterinarians removed the beasts that had plagued him through the long night. Monitoring the action with strained blurry eyes, he lay as still as a slab of concrete.

Malena refused to leave, not even after the others arrived and told her to step out. She shook her head. "I'm not leaving." When free, he'd kiss his sweetheart breathless.

One by one. Each time the handler lifted a snake

and put it into a cage, Dustin experienced less pressure on his body. A lengthy process but the torment would soon be over.

At least this torment.

"Guys, keep searching even after you think they are all captured," Dustin demanded.

Released from bondage, he could breathe. Praise the Lord.

When he received the all clear, he climbed from the bed then stood still to regain his equilibrium before turning toward Malena and her comforting arms.

Tori woke with a horrible headache. The words—car accident—reverberated through her brain. The last thing she clearly remembered—being at home and the phone conversation with Malena.

Vague fuzzy images of people working on her with loud excited voices pulsed through her mind. She heard the words, "car wreck" and puffed out a breath. More unclear visions to add to her brain files.

Careful not to move her head too much, she took in her surroundings—a brightly lit screened-off cubicle with her on a bed in the center. Hospital? Tori wore a faded hospital gown and a blood pressure cuff circled her upper right arm. An IV went into her left arm. Pillows propped up her splinted right leg. The tiniest movement caused pain in her leg and head. She forced herself to lie still. Why and how did she get there?

A hand pushed the curtain back and a woman in scrubs approached. "I'm Doctor Sara Kim. They said you were awake. That's a good sign. We had a precarious night deciding what antivenom to use. Do you know what kind of snake attacked you?"

"Snake? What are you talking about? They told me I was in a car crash. I wasn't around any snakes."

"Look at your left hand."

Tori tilted her head, winced as she lifted her arm attached to the IV, and saw a swollen mass with two puncture marks on her bruised hand. She gasped and lowered her arm. "I don't know. I thought I survived an accident."

"You did. And you're fortunate. They called it a nasty crash. According to the paramedics, you vomited and lost consciousness. Either could've caused the crash. We detected the bite and delivered polyvalent snake antivenom to you. We were lucky we chose the right serum and your body responded immediately. Along with the snakebite, your leg is fractured. When swelling subsides, you'll receive a cast. An orthopedist is scheduled to see you later and will go over all that entails. The head injury and snakebite took precedence. We're still monitoring the trauma to your skull and cheekbone. I'll check on you later. Your nurse will be back in to help you with your meal."

"Thank you."

The doctor left and slid the curtain back, shielding her from the world. Her mind roved around the last few days, including the terrible interrogation yesterday when she thought they would arrest her. What if they found out she knew Anna? She lied to the police—Malena's man. Worse, she yelled at her friend who always supported her. What about her car? A snakebite? Where did she encounter a snake? Did someone put it in her car? Tori's life unraveled like pulling a thread on a loose weave sweater. A tear slid down her cheek. Afraid to move, she didn't wipe it away. Let it come. She deserved a good cry.

"Are you okay?" Dustin held Malena. Tears rolled down her beautiful face.

She spoke against his chest. "Me? I should ask you. How dreadful."

In his arms, he felt her quivering. "You stayed. All that time, you stayed. Thank you, honey. The last few weeks have been tough. I'm sorry about my distance toward you. When this is over, I want us to get married. I know it's on the calendar but I want to move it up and live our lives together. What do you say?"

"I agree. This puts everything into perspective."

Dustin and Malena stepped back but remained close, holding hands. "I'm packing and going to a hotel until we know for a fact that no more reptiles hide ready to attack." He shuddered. "They'll set traps or something to reassure me before I move back in."

"Let's get married now. That'd solve the problem."

"Elope? No. You've waited for a big wedding with family and friends and all the frills money can buy. I want you to have the best memories to pass down to our children and grandchildren. Anyway, the Lord assured me I needed to stay the course on this case. He will help me.

"But first things first. How did the snakes get in? The many different species means intent and a break-in. My team didn't find anything to suggest a forced entry.

I thought about your doorbell camera. I don't have one but what if there's a camera that captured us using the code to get into the garage? Come with me." Not wanting to let go of her hand, he kept it as they went to the front of his house.

Dustin stood with his back to the garage door keypad and scanned the street and the house across from it. "There." He pointed to the tree in his adjoining neighbor's yard. Letting go of her hand, he strode forward, a shudder of nerves running down his back. A renewed sense of determination and protectiveness gripped him not only for his loved ones but also for the community. "There's something in the birdhouse and it doesn't have feathers."

Back at his garage, he found a ladder to lean against the tree. Malena used both hands to steady the ladder. Up he went and moved the fake nesting material. "Gotcha."

"I didn't expect that. Very good." The man quirked his thin lips. "You think you're smart. Not smart enough. You didn't find them all." Laughter brought on a wheeze.

Before him on the screens, drama played out of McCall discovering a camera and his crew taking it down then disconnecting the leads which caused the man's screen to go black. Oh bother. He switched to another camera to monitor the detective. This one didn't give him a close-up. From across the street, another doorbell cam showed Officer Kent handing

McCall a bag. Blue showed through the clear plastic. “They found the note.” His lips stretched tight.

Stone-faced, McCall viewed the message and handed it back.

Another officer approached with a small bag in her hand. The man couldn’t see what she’d bagged nor heard what they said. He watched, intent on reading the symphony of body language. “Not even riled, detective. Ah, but your girlfriend isn’t so good at hiding her emotions.”

Excitement mounted. The man gave a toothy grin and rubbed his fingers against his palms.

Chapter 18

"Honey, I'm sorry." Dustin held Malena as she shook her head and trembled. "Evidence is trickling in and I need to stay objective. I know you love Tori and want to protect her but the jewel they found appears to be the same as the ones on her watch. You recognized it." He pulled away and with his finger tilted her chin up to see her face. "Listen, it may not be hers."

She nodded and sighed. "I know. I'm praying it's just a terrible mistake. A jewel from someone else's jewelry on your bedroom floor."

"Ouch. That sounds bad."

Malena quirked a smile. "Now, I don't know which is worse, Tori or some other woman in your room."

"Either way. Snakes didn't decide to invade my home. A jewel-wearing perpetrator put them there. I'll escort you home and see you safe inside. Then I'll follow up on leads."

"Dusty, you didn't sleep last night."

"For the first few hours, I did. I normally sleep hard so I don't need much but last night I crashed. Almost comatose." He frowned. Someone slip him a Mickey? "Hm. That's why I didn't hear the stealth serpent bearers. We'll drive through and get breakfast and coffees on the way."

"In separate cars. How romantic." She lifted an eyebrow.

Dustin laughed and slipped his arm around her. "That's my girl."

He escorted Malena to her car then climbed into his SUV to follow.

After searching and clearing her house, he headed to the last crime scene.

Yellow bands across a sealed door greeted him. Grimacing, he ducked through the yellow X and used his knife on the adhesive tape over the doorjamb to let himself in. "Detective McCall." His voice echoed through the expansive entry.

The house should be empty. No answer. He surveyed the room and peered up to what was left of the bracket and wires that once held the ginormous chandelier. Dustin nodded and took the stairs two at a time to the second-floor balcony.

Dustin studied the spans below. The view. He turned around to search for the perfect spot for a camera.

A smoke detector caught his eye. Scooting down the stairs, he went to his vehicle for the compact telescopic ladder. Back upstairs, he opened it and leaned it against the wall beside the detector. The cover easily came off and he uncovered the small lens. Climbing down, he pulled out his phone. "Kent, get forensics to Anna Buckingham's. We need to check all the other homes for cameras. In the smoke detectors. Cameras are hidden in plain sight. I found one with a wide view of the entry and murder spot. I'm sure there are more. I want all the tiny cameras found at every address. Also, send a crew to search my house. We didn't check in the perfect place to hide them, inside smoke detectors. Everyone sees these alarms but ignores them until they chirp or sound off. I bet the batteries are fresh in the detectors too.

"This explains the murderer's perfect timing. The guy must carry a compact computer to watch as he monitors the people before he initiates his plan and final moves. He'd know everyone's whereabouts in the house as he loosened the screws and set the charge. Kent, he's watching. The perp knows I found this one." Goosebumps erupted on Dustin's arms and the hairs on his neck stood up.

Kent's voice floated through the phone. "A notice came in that our suspect ended up in the hospital in the wee hours of the morning. Her car crashed into a tree. But get this. Victoria was snake bit."

Dustin whistled. "Got her."

"Appears so. Sir, I should've listened to you. I'm on my way to arrest her. Unless you want to do the honors?"

"I'm driving to Doctor Harper's house. He's my number one suspect. You handle Victoria. She's not alone in this deadly game."

At Doctor Harper's address, he parked perpendicular once again to block the three-car driveway. Overdue for another visit with the doc. His phone vibrated and sounded the familiar overture. "Malena, you all right?"

"Yes. Dusty, Tori is in the hospital. She got in an accident last night and couldn't be the one."

The tone of her voice told him to be careful how he

responded. “Babe. How is she?”

“Banged up. Broken leg and concussion. She hit a tree.”

“Ouch. That’s bad. I need to tell you Kent called me. We were notified. Also, did she tell you a snake bit her?”

“What?” Malena’s voice sounded breathless.

Dustin waited while she processed the information.

“No.”

In the simple word, he heard abrupt dejection like when a high-flying kite plummets to the ground after the wind dies.

“I’m sorry.” Those two words, his gut told him, would be spoken many times in the coming days. The foreseeable problem—he’d have to arrest his fiancée’s old college roommate and close friend.

Dustin pushed the doorbell button. Doctor Harper answered on the fourth chime, wearing boxer shorts and a loosely tied black robe. His rumpled hair sticking out in all directions and red-rimmed watery eyes spoke of a bleak night. Dustin made a point of looking at his watch. Eleven thirty-three. “I’m glad to catch you home, Doctor Harper. I have a few questions for you. Mind if I come in?”

The doctor left the door open, turned, and staggered inside. Dustin entered, closed the door, and followed him to the living room. His host plopped down on an overstuffed chair and picked up an insulated cup, taking a drink. Adjacent to the chair sat a long couch where Dustin perched, resting his forearms on his knees and leaned forward to look Harper in the eyes. “Rough night?” The guy looked terrible. Soused?

“You could say that. I got a flat tire out on the mesa.” He grabbed a tissue from a box, blew his nose, then tossed it in an overflowing basket beside the chair. “My cell phone died, so I hoofed it home.”

“Bummer. Didn’t feel like changing it yourself?” What a wimp.

“My jack was missing.”

“Missing?” Yeah, right. “Have you used it before?”

“No. Never checked for one. I just presumed it came with one.” He shrugged. “It’s part of the truck. You know? Look, I don’t make sure all the bearings and wires and stuff are there. When you purchase, you assume it’s all intact.” He screwed up his face. “Geez. What’s this all about?”

“Get it towed?” Did he rehearse this?

“I called for a tow truck and left a message.”

“What time?”

He hissed out a breath. “I arrived home around three this morning.”

Dustin nodded. “Want me to take you to your vehicle?”

“They’ll deliver it. I decided to have it serviced and a car jack put in. Anyway, I own two other modes of transportation.”

“Speaking of transportation, I understand you purchased a motorized man lift. Why would you need one of those?”

The doctor ran his hands over his face, then rubbed his eyes with the heels of his hands. “Why all the questions? Why do you need to know?"

"I'm in the middle of a murder investigation." He pointed at him and his voice raised. "Your patients are the targets. Not answering my questions makes you look guilty and bumps you up on the suspect list."

Controlling his anger, Dustin lowered his volume back to a friendly chat. "Answer my questions here, unless you're craving a cup of stale coffee at headquarters?" Dustin settled against the cushions and draped his arm over the back of the sofa. Waited and watched the emotions flicker across the doctor's face.

Confusion marked by worry lines spread across Harper's forehead and he bit his lip, then his eyes darted back and forth across the ceiling as if searching for an answer.

Dustin wondered if he would capitulate?

Harper took another long sip from the cup. "It helps me." He tapped his knee and traced his finger down an old scar on his kneecap. "The weather can be bothersome."

Dustin stared deadpan at the suspect. Which one helped him? The man lift or the drink he swigs? Both?

The doctor fidgeted.

The detective sat tight. Let him sweat.

He sighed and nodded. "You probably want to see it. All right, I'll show you."

Dustin rose and waited for the doctor to commit, then followed.

Down the hall, they passed a room where a huge table held a jigsaw puzzle in the process of completion. The box's lid showed a picture of the Sistine Chapel. Dustin whistled. "That must take you a while."

"What?" He turned. "Oh. Yeah, I like to do puzzles

to clear my mind. When I'm not out in the wilderness, I do that. I watch T.V. and put the pieces together."

"Broncos or Rockies?"

The doctor shook his head and took another drink. "I like crime shows."

I bet. "How many pieces?" Dustin lifted the box. "Eighteen thousand. That's ambitious. How long does it take you?"

"My ex-wife and kids come over and help sometimes, so it doesn't take years. My brother stays here from time to time, in fact the leech left yesterday. If he'd stayed one more day, he could've picked me up last night. The bum." He emitted a bitter chuckle and he kept walking.

Interesting. He doesn't like his brother. He's divorced. Dustin put a piece in place. Satisfied, he turned to follow the doctor. They passed an elevator door. This house needed an elevator? Dustin whistled. "Got yourself an elevator. That's pretty cool. I bet it makes it easier to move furniture up there."

"Down too. It goes to the basement and the second floor." He nodded. "And yes, it made it easier putting the pool table and hot tub in. Also, my mother-in-law needed it when she lived here." He swigged his drink and continued down the hall.

In the garage, the object stood like a sentry in front of the smaller, single-bay garage door and a motorcycle parked behind it. Did he use the man lift more than the bike?

Harper waved his hand to the wall covered in shelves from floor to ceiling, holding large rectangular crates. All gray. All the exact size. All in precise spacing.

"Christmas decorations. Yeah. I'm one of those."

Dustin flipped through his memory and snapped his fingers. "This is the house. The one all done up that blinks to music during the holidays." He whistled. "Nice." Turning his attention to the subject of the inquiry, he pointed to the lift. "This?"

"It helps me reach these." He pointed to the crates. "I don't need to climb a ladder and balance the crates while climbing down. Also, I access the roof to hang decorations and I have a place up there where I like to put my tripod and camera to take pictures of the mountains and sky, especially the night sky."

Dustin adjusted his Stetson. "How high does the lift extend?"

"Forty feet?" Harper scratched his scruffy chin and took another drink.

"More than adequate."

Harper frowned. "Yes. Why? Is there a problem that I use a lift?"

"What mechanic has your truck?"

"What? Oh. DC Auto Repair on Main. Going to check on my alibi? Do I need one? Did someone else die?"

"Correct on all accounts."

"Who?"

"Since we last talked, another patient of yours, Anna Buckingham."

"Oh, um." He blinked his eyes in rapid succession. "That's terrible. Cute girl. I didn't kill her either. I healed her."

"So you say. We need to verify." Dustin leaned in. "Anyone see you walking last night?"

"A few cars. He shrugged. "No one stopped for

me. I didn't get a good look at them, either."

Dustin clicked his tongue. "So, again, your movements are unsubstantiated."

He frowned and squinted his eyes as if in pain, rubbed his chin, and took another swig of his drink. "Pretty much."

"Doctor, you don't have an alibi for any of the times tragedy hits Durango. Should I lock you up so no one else dies or to confirm you aren't the culprit?"

Lifting his head Harper said through clinched teeth, "You can't do that on a hunch. This interview is over. Leave. I'll not talk to you again without my attorney present." He pushed the garage opener and thumbed out the growing opening. Dustin had no choice but to leave. Two steps out, the metal door descended.

"What a jerk." Dustin climbed into his SUV, started it, and studied the suspect's house. "Secrets live there." Harper didn't even ask who got murdered. Because he knows? Or doesn't care?

Annoyed at Harper, Dustin wanted to throw the book at him. He rolled his eyes. Not enough evidence.

A wide sidewalk circled around the house. Easy to drive the man lift on. Putting the SUV in gear, he drove twenty miles an hour around the block. Between two houses, he located Harper's roof and the platform that would hold a tripod and a man. Dustin whistled. Two suspects, both with platforms on their roofs for viewing the world around them. "What are the odds?"

Chapter 19

Crutches propped Tori as she maneuvered through the hospital hallway. She sported a cast from toe to mid-thigh. The male tech ambled beside her, making sure she used the aluminum supports with confidence. Planting them, her arms took much of her weight but her swollen hand throbbed, causing her to grit her teeth. Never bitten before, she didn't know it could hurt like it did.

"Are you sure you don't want a motorized chair? I can get you one."

"This is better for my lifestyle." She wished all of this to be a bad dream.

He nodded at her hand. "The swelling might take a while to go down."

"They already told me," Tori grunted. "I'll be fine."

At the end of the hall, she turned around to head back to her room. Halfway there, he pointed toward her hospital room door. "Looks like someone's waiting for you."

Tori lifted her head. Officer Kent. Her stomach flipped and a smile broadened across her face.

As she drew near, the look on his features made

her hesitate. She wobbled and almost fell but the strong hand of the tech steadied her. “Easy there.”

At the door, she stopped. “Officer Kent. Is this a friendly visit?”

“Sorry, Ms. Miller, I need to take you in. I’m not going to cuff you, but Victoria Miller, you are under arrest for breaking and entering into Detective McCall’s residence and endangering his life. You have the right to remain s….”

Tori came to and blinked a few times, catching glimpses of her surroundings. What happened? She observed her position from the bed in the hospital room. Fear cascaded through her, causing a racing heart. How and when did she end up back in bed? Handcuffs fastened her good arm to the bed rail. She jangled it. Yep, locked. Head elevated with an oxygen mask affixed over her nose and mouth. Her last memory blasted in like a zephyr against the sails on a ship.

Arrested?

“Glad you’re with us. We’ll need to keep you for observation at least for a few more hours since you fainted. How do you feel?”

Tori turned her head to see an older nurse standing next to a monitor for vital signs with straight lines and no numbers. Her cheerful green scrubs with pelicans dancing across the material seemed a stark contrast to the somber situation. Pulling up the oxygen mask, she said, “Strange. Can I take this off?”

“Not yet. Here. Put this on, so I can see your levels.” The nurse clipped a little monitor on her index finger. “Let me get your blood pressure.” She pushed a button on the automatic machine, which started humming, and the arm cuff tightened. “It’s a good thing that nice, and easy on the eyes, officer caught you or you'd have a nasty bump on your head next to the bruise you already sport. Um, ha." The nurse smirked and nodded her tightly curled black-haired head.

Tori liked her.

Badge out, Dustin approached the mechanic who had Doctor Harper's vehicle on the hydraulic lift. "Excuse me, I'm investigating a case. I need a word."

The man came out from under the five-thousand-pound hunk of steel and wiped his grimy hands on a soiled cloth. He eyed the badge. "What do you want to know?"

Dustin read his name patch. "Emmett, how did you get this SUV?"

He scratched his head, squinted, then hollered behind him. "Hey, Phil."

A guy in matching stained coveralls with greasy hair and smudges on his face swaggered over.

"You towed the doc's ride here?" Emmett thumbed at the car behind him in the air.

"Right." He spoke through gray teeth. "This mornin'. T.J. lifted the info off the message. 'Twas right where s'posed to be."

"Do you know the time of the message?" Dustin asked.

Phil shrugged. "Bout three-thirty?"

"What did the tire look like? Nail in it?"

"Nope." Phil's matted, long hair looked like a helmet.

"Explain."

"Flat, man. De. . . fla. . . ted." His head bobbed at every syllable. "Water didn't bubble. Nope. Nothin' wrong a little air didn't fix. Inflated it, tis all. Someone messed with it. Yep, done on purpose." He spat a dark brown stream of chew into a trash can to his right.

"Gotcha." Dustin cocked his head at Emmett. "Find a tire jack?"

He shook his head. "Nope. Strange, right? Who doesn't have a jack in these mountains where anything can mess with a tire? Sharp rock. Pothole." He clicked his tongue. "Heck, a few years ago, someone got a tire shot during hunting season. Never drive without one myself."

Dustin nodded. "True. Can I see the bracket where it should be?"

Phil hovered nearby. Emmett pushed the button for the hydraulics to lower. Once the vehicle rested on the ground, he opened the rear door sporting a rugged tire. "No bracket. Just a nice hidey-hole for it." He popped it open. "There."

Dustin shined his flashlight in the long narrow compartment located inside and found it empty. "Clean." No dust. No marks. "Can you tell if this thing ever held a jack?"

Emmett frowned as he examined it. "Not sure. But even with the cover snapped into place, with all the off-road stuff he does. . . it should have a little dirt. The rubber mat is a tad dirty. There's dust and grime here." He pointed a grungy fingernail at the track the door rested in when closed. Next to it sat the empty compartment that should hold the tools to remove the tire from the back of the door, jack up the vehicle, and loosen or tighten the lugs. Dustin took pictures of everything and dusted for prints. “You’ve been most helpful.”

Chapter 20

Jail? The eight-by-six cubicle held a sink, a toilet, and a bunk bed. How did her life become so messed up?

Tori's only option—hop. At least she didn't have far to go in the tight space. They'd confiscated her crutches, assuming she'd use them as a weapon. How could she? Standing took all her strength and balance so the thought of using the crutch as a weapon—preposterous.

Her broken leg hurt from the jostling while hopping. The cast weighed a ton. Lying down on the lower bunk, she propped her leg on a pillow. Misery threatened to overcome her. Who would…who could ever love her now? According to them, she was a criminal. Fingerprinted again and they posed her for a mug shot. She shivered. Cold. Abandoned. Unloved.

The intermittent sounds of the modernized automated doors swishing open and closed, footsteps, and an occasional muffled voice from around the building faded away as she stepped deep into her thoughts, replaying the last few weeks over and over. Houses and other residences flashed in her brain. Darkness overshadowed light. Conversations mingled into a garbled mess. Thoughts like spaghetti muddled and twisted in her brain. Tension, fatigue, and sore muscles all grouped against her to wear her down.

The throbbing in her hand increased her anxiety. Using her fingers, Tori examined the bandage. Her head swirled with unanswered questions. How did a snake bite her? The mystery of the car crash. How did it happen? That entire night's memories were wiped from her brain.

She closed her eyes as her hand went to the tender spot on her head and traced down to the swelling on her check, wishing she remembered what happened.

The door slid open. She startled and lifted her eyes. The guard didn't enter but stood right beyond the doorway. "You have a visitor. Malena Campbell."

Her heart lurched. Tori struggled to her feet. What would Malena say?

To keep balance, she rested her hand on his forearm as she hopped down the long corridor. Didn't they have a wheelchair? She didn't deserve the courtesy.

He took her into the room for visitors. Relief washed over her. She imagined the room would be like she'd seen on TV where the prisoner talked through a window. Instead, seated on the other side of a small table, Malena and her radiant grin greeted her. Tori took a deep, shaky breath and her lips quivered into a slight smile. "Malena." She eased down in the chair across from her friend.

Malena leaned forward, meeting her eyes. "Hi girl."

The sweet voice undid her. A tear escaped Tori's eye. She scraped it away. Why cry? It wouldn't help.

The guard stood in front of the now-closed door, still in her peripheral vision. He could hear whatever they talked about.

"How ya doing?" Malena's voice sounded soft and kind.

She shrugged. "Fine, I guess."

"I wish I could talk to you about this predicament." Malena waved her hand to encompass the room and beyond.

Tori leaned forward with her good hand palm open and up, and pleaded for an answer. "Why is God doing this to me?"

"That's a fair question. I don't have all the answers but I think He's allowing this for your benefit."

Frowning, Tori slammed herself back into her chair. "What? Are you kidding? How?" Malena's words stung. Why wasn't she on her side?

"If you're innocent, Tori, and I hope you are, I think you're somehow tangled in a web and God wants you to talk to Him to get untangled. Trust Him. Ask Him. You felt certain God gave you the revelations of the crime scenes. You wanted to help. You thought you were helping. But there's more to this whole thing. Tori, God didn't give you the visions. Why would He do it *after* the murders? How could that help? It couldn't prevent them. I believe He wants to help you, and to help Dustin solve these murders and put the person behind bars, but you have to ask Him."

Tori wrapped her arms around herself. "I'm frightened. I don't remember anything. They are accusing me of things that I can't prove wrong because I don't remember and can't come up with an alibi. I don't remember any of the crash or the snake or anything of the night. I don't understand why I get these visions. If what you're saying is true, how am I involved? I. . ." Tears poured unbidden down her face.

Malena pushed tissues over. "I wish I could hug you. I've been praying for you every day. In one of my prayers, I received a word from the Lord for you."

Tori hiccupped—crying brought them on. She snatched three tissues and mopped her face. "What?" She held her breath.

Malena pointed up. "He says, 'you need to trust Me. Not just know of Me. Begin a relationship with Me.'"

Tori stilled. The hiccups stopped. Malena's words stung yet calmed her. "A relationship? I can't go to church. I'm locked in here." She shrugged.

"Church is beside the point. You need to ask for forgiveness for all the mess-ups and bad stuff. Bare your heart, trust God, trust Jesus, and ask Him into your life. It won't get you out of here but it will ease the burden you're carrying."

Drowning in a sea of despair, Malena sent her a life raft. She needed to reach out and take it. Should she? Could she?

In the interrogation room, Dustin put his tablet down on the desk and plopped a folder next to it. Victoria, wearing a two-piece short-sleeved prisoner issued canvas outfit—missing a pant leg cut off for her cast—sat across the desk. He took the chair beside Kent. "We've got more evidence. You still say you didn't drive yourself into the tree?"

"I can't remember anything." She pulled her good leg up with her heel on the seat of the chair, hugged her leg, and rested her chin on her knee.

A protective posture. As close to a fetal position as possible.

He swiped his tablet and swiveled it to face her. "Here is your car. When we took a still and blew it up, it showed you behind the wheel. Now—" He swiped again. "Here's the video we found at the 7-Eleven across from your accident. Watch and tell me what you see."

Tori leaned in close past her knee to view the screen.

In a moment, she jerked back, dropped her leg, and covered her mouth with a shaking hand. Her face went pale.

"Well? Describe what happened."

"I. . ." Tears streamed.

Kent slid a box of tissues to her.

She grabbed a few and swiped at the fountain. "The driver turned the car toward the t…tree." Her shoulders convulsed. Whimpers accompanied the jerking movements. The crying didn't move Dustin. He'd seen it all before. Could this be an act?

"Who drove?"

She stomped her foot and groaned. "I drove."

Dustin pointed at her. "Yes. You deliberately drove your car into that oak. Why?"

She shook her head. "I d…don't know."

"Okay." Dustin seized a picture of her bejeweled watch from the folder and slipped it toward her giving her a good look. "Is this yours?"

Tori nodded. "My watch."

He pointed. "See? Missing a jewel."

She nodded.

"Try to explain this." He slapped an evidence bag containing a tiny, clear, crystal jewel in front of her. "It's confirmed it came from your watch. It ended up on *my bedroom floor*. Illuminate me."

She winced. Terror etched her face. Her body vibrated as she violently shook her head. Her teeth chattered and she stuttered. "I've never been in your house. S…someone p…planted it." She hiccupped.

"Oh, so someone is framing you? That's rich."

An alert on his phone notified Dustin of new information coming in.

Dustin scooped up the evidence and stood. "Think of another explanation." He'd leave her to stew on their findings. Kent took the clue and followed, closing the door.

Dustin led them to their shared office. "The techs found something inside her watch." At the computer, he read the report stating the watch contained what amounted to a two-way communications device. Out loud he processed what he read, "A listener could hear everything, including what we've said while it was in our possession. Also, the device made it possible for someone to talk to the wearer of the watch. Good thing the Techs disconnected it. He whistled. "Can they do that?" Swiveling the chair, he regarded his partner. "Technology, I mean."

"Seems so. I've read about communication devices but I didn't know they were advanced to that level."

"The mastermind. Can we trace it to know who's talking to her?"

"They're working on it."

Dustin stood and studied the board. The six innocent victims' eyes pleaded with him to avenge their dreadful deaths. These six didn't deserve any of their suffering and deaths. The numbers were staggering and they didn't include the threat to Jim, Malena, and himself.

At first, he investigated the deaths of strangers, but it became personal when Jim ended up in the hospital. Then his friend Ted became a casualty. More strangers became targets and their pictures added to the board. Next, the scumbag targeted his sweetheart Malena, and more recently himself.

To muck up the water, Victoria Miller, Malena's close college friend, found herself in the middle. Dustin added her mugshot next to the DMV pictures of Doctor Harper and Professor Olson. Did the culprit kill each person shrinking the circle to Dustin as the target all along? A tangled web the culprit weaved. What part did the madman play? The spider? The cat? "Well buddy—" He flicked each of the three pictures with his finger. "The spider or the cat will be caught and prosecuted."

He turned back to his desk. The picture of the watch caught his attention. "Kent, we need to ask her where she got the watch."

Back in the interrogation room, Dustin and Kent found Tori with her head on her arm atop the table. "Excuse us, were you sleeping?"

She jerked up, eyes wide. "I, uh…no. Praying."

"You should." Dustin nodded to his partner then leaned against the wall, in a non-threatening stance.

Kent took the seat in front of her. "Where did you get your watch?"

She sniffed and offered a weak smile. "It was the coolest thing. This survey came in the mail saying to fill it out by a certain time and I could win a prize. A few weeks later, the watch came." She leaned back in her chair and beamed at Kent as if she'd won a twenty-million-dollar lotto ticket.

"Do you have any paperwork or the package it came in?"

She shrugged. "That's been around a year ago." She scrunched her face and shook her head. "I'm sure I threw it away."

"Did it come with the band or did you change it out?"

"I liked it the way it came with my favorite colors and just enough bling but not overdone. I would've picked it out myself. Perfect. I synced it with my phone. It captures my workouts and everything. Before then, I didn't realize how many footsteps I got in. Can I have it back?"

"Not while you're here. A guard will escort you to your cell."

"Release you mean. I've cooperated with you and you've not charged me. You need to release me."

"You're charged with breaking and entering."

She crossed her arms. "Then I don't want to talk anymore."

Kent stood. Dustin led the way and stopped to speak to an officer. "Ms. Miller requests to be escorted back to her cell."

Chapter 21

On the computer in the office, Dustin found the report on the murder of Anna Buckingham. His cheeks puffed from a deep breath and he exhaled as slow as sorghum. Fingerprints were from the gardener, the housekeeper, and the victim. Not a trace of anyone not supposed to be there, except for the tracks left by the manlift. He'd need a search warrant to match the tread.

"Kent, what do you make of the Buckingham file?"

"Yeah, I read they discovered hydrochloric acid on the bracket pieces found amongst the debris."

"Also used in the shower murder."

"Yep. And, the pieces you pointed out came from a timing device that emitted a fast acting acid."

"Anna didn't have a chance." What a diabolical mind. Had he met the culprit? Or had his gut led him to the wrong conclusions? Someone drove the lift and set a timer for the acid to pour on the metal. Timing. Exact. A genius. Each murder shouted a brilliant though deviant mind.

"Detective, her house was too isolated. We didn't find any cameras from other sources to observe the culprit, but we found numerous cameras inside her house and on her property pointing to the home as you suspected, but the killer owns those recordings. I wonder if he revisits what he witnessed."

Dustin checked his watch. In a few hours, another person would die if he didn't intercept the next murder. "They found a blue card at my house but no one died."

"I think you were supposed to."

The memory remained sharp in his mind. His stomach flipped and his hands perspired. "The night lasted forever. When did the killer start his timer to tick down to zero from forty-eight hours?"

"And how did they know you were afraid of snakes?"

Dustin interlaced his fingers behind his head, leaned back in his seat, hearing the familiar creak of his chair. "My guess is he saw my reaction to the stairway murder where they caught that viper. I didn't know we were being watched." He closed his eyes. "Or I wouldn't have given him the benefit."

Kent chuckled. "If you could've controlled your terror."

Laughter exploded. Dustin permitted himself to laugh good and long, needing a way to release some of the tension.

On the computer, he pulled up the long list obtained from a court-ordered warrant. "You have a copy of the doctor's patient list?"

Kent riffled through files on his computer. "Yep."

"I had no idea the doctor treated so many residents of Durango and surrounding towns. Recognize any names?"

"Not so far."

"We need to focus on those living within the city

limits and stretch it out to a ten-mile radius." Frustration mounting, he blew out his cheeks in a slow exhale. Small towns equaled limited resources and manpower to protect all the names. One by one, he read down the list. He frowned. Senna Parker. Turning to his computer, he did a search on her. The picture of a young woman seemed familiar. He snapped his fingers.

"Find something?" Kent rolled his chair over to Dustin's desk to peer over his shoulder at the screen.

"Maybe. I attended her wedding. Malena looked amazing as a bride's maid. Rex. Yes. That's right. She married a guy named Rex." Another of Malena's friends. Should he send someone over? To say what? You may or may not be a target? Elicit more panic? Did he have an alternative?

The white walled room with rows of monitors, the audience—the man appraising what he witnessed. "You're a busy little detective visiting people and following your leads. Will it be enough to catch me? I think not. You've no idea what I'm capable of. This plan has been worked and reworked for years. The mathematics and design are perfect. The added game of snake and mouse amuses me. I've never enjoyed as much fun as watching you sweat. Let me assure you, your brain is no match for mine." Frustration sprinkled through his body. The monitors provided only silent movies but it couldn't be helped.

He focused on one screen, then another, and another until all the players, on each of the ten addresses, were accounted for. A long pull on the ever-present drink settled his emotions and a craggy smirk filled his face.

Stakeout. Dustin and Kent sat low in the seats of an old truck. Not wanting to be recognized, they arrived in the rust-infested 1996 two-door. The truck's exterior gave an impression of a machine not able to get out of its own way, but the body was the only thing old. Everything that mattered dated 2019 or newer, including the chassis, interior, state-of-the-art-radio, right down to the rugged tires. This baby looked its three decades but could chase another vehicle and haul up a rugged mountain if needed.

Before the sun went down, they parked three blocks away. Darkness descended hours ago. Would his hunch pay off or did they waste precious time?

Kent whispered, "Part of me hopes the culprit doesn't show. Not knowing what his schemes are this time gives me the willies but on the other hand, we could catch him."

In the dark, Dustin nodded. "Boredom and physical needs on stakeouts bring doubts and frustration. I'm praying no one gets hurt and we catch this guy to put an end to the mayhem. Not telling Senna and Rex that they may be in danger makes me sweat and gives me indigestion."

"Exactly." Kent sighed.

Headlights headed from a side street and switched off before the car turned away from them. Interesting.

"Got something." Dustin pulled the binoculars up to his eyes. A nondescript compact entered the cul-de-sac and parked near the address.

The door on the driver's side opened. A figure all in black, with not a patch of skin showing, climbed out in a crouch and made a beeline to the back of the house. "Gotcha."

Active screens played out before him. The man took a swig from his drink and watched his plan unfold, movie by movie. Satisfied, he nodded. "Now, onto my next victim." On each hand, he rubbed the pads of his fingers against his thumbs in excitement. He whispered into his microphone. "Good job. Now remember, stealth is the key and silence is golden. Sneak in and proceed as planned. I'm listening and watching." He turned off his microphone and regarded his worker entering the dark residence and creeping into the kitchen. The man strained for any noise his worker might make as his lips searched out the straw, sucked, and swallowed.

After a few minutes, the screen in front of him showed the poison being introduced into the water line. The needle would make a pinhole leak, but death would happen before it became a concern.

He chuckled then switched on the microphone. "Good. Wipe it clean." He took a drink. "That's right. Now slide…" Movement in another screen caught his eye, so quick, he almost didn't catch it. The man frowned and scanned the other monitors. Nothing. Did he imagine it?

He refocused on his worker. “Slide the appliance back and gather . . .” Lights came on in the kitchen of the video. “What?”

His opponent appeared. “McCall? No!” He quickly switched off his microphone as anguished cries escaped his lips. Sweat popped out of his forehead. His mind didn’t want to acknowledge what played out in front of him. How did the incompetent detective figure it out? The man’s world went helter-skelter.

Chapter 22

Dustin jumped from his office chair and sprinted the six steps to the door. "Jim? What are you doing here?" He clasped his old friend's hand and pumped it. "You look great. I'm sorry, buddy, I haven't been by to check on you."

"Slow down, Dustin, my boy." Jim sat in Dustin's chair and leaned back, causing it to squeak. "I love that sound." He rubbed his hands over the well-worn wood on the armrests. "I'm doing fine. How are you? I heard something about your imprisonment." He quirked a smile.

Dustin's hand covered his grin and rubbed his cheeks. "So, you heard."

"I learned you sweated bullets during the reptile occupation and your woman stood by you through the extraction process."

Dustin cringed. "Malena talked to Jenny."

Jim nodded and swiveled to look at his old desk. "How's your new partner?"

"He fits and we work well together. An asset."

"Hope he's a good listener."

Dustin chuckled. "Ha ha. So, Jim, what brought you in?"

"This." He pulled out his phone. "Earlier, I told my sweetie I needed to get out and walk. I ended up on Ted and Willow's street and came across an elderly neighbor who let me look through her video feed. I caught this." He swung the phone for Dustin to see a video of a person clad in black wearing a hoodie drop off an identical box to the one Ted opened. The murder weapon.

"Our guys canvassed the neighbors. How'd you get this?"

"Years back, I got her son out of a jam." Jim handed him a cable.

"I'll ask the tech guys if they can clean this up." He used the cable to connect the phone to the computer and downloaded the video. "Sometimes technology is helpful but other times deadly."

"Same coin. Two sides."

"Unfortunately. On the side of justice, your timing is perfect. We're holding a man who's cooling his heels in interrogation. This might make his lips spill into a confession. We intercepted him injecting cyanide into the refrigerator's drinking line."

"Oh, Lord Almighty." He rubbed a shaky hand over his mouth and shuddered.

"Don't worry. All's well. The techs are flushing and installing new lines as we speak. We're hosting the targets in an out-of-town hotel until we apprehend the mastermind. I'm headed to interrogate the suspect. Want to watch?"

Jim shook his head. "I promised I'd stay out of it. Don't want to stack my lies. I already need to head home and tell the missus about getting the video for you."

Dustin squeezed the older man's shoulder. "Thanks Jim. Give her and daughter thank you kisses from me."

Dustin, armed with multiple video evidence, met Kent at the door to interrogation. Earlier, they consumed a fortifying breakfast. "Did you get the video I sent?"

"Yeah. Same build as our guy. Solid evidence. Hope this makes him sing."

"Ready?"

"Yep." Kent held up a sack.

"Leave that here." Dustin opened the door and walked in. "Yep. Eggs, sausage, toast, and hash browns." He took a chair and placed his tablet on the table. "A large orange juice and coffee."

"Did you try the cinnamon rolls? Hot out of the oven, gooey and dripping icing." Kent pulled out the remaining chair and straddled it.

"Oh, man, I missed those. Hot and gooey?" Dustin snapped his fingers. "Shoot." He glanced at the perpetrator they arrested last night and recognized the pained, hungry look. Good. Let him feel the need for food. "I'll drop back by the restaurant to get some of those and I heard their pie is unbelievable. Flaky crust and any flavor you can imagine. À la mode too." He rubbed his stomach. "Not sure I have room."

"There's always room for pie and ice cream." Kent took a large swallow from the coffee he'd brought with him. "Their coffee is excellent, too."

"Smooth." Dustin lit up his tablet and turned it facing their handcuffed guest, Jackson Black. "We've caught you on video delivering a box with another lethal dose to an innocent man." He pushed play.

Jackson looked at it and shook his head. "Not me."

"Sure it is."

The perp leaned back and rested his conjoined wrists on his thighs as if he didn't have a care in the world. His rap sheet showed numerous encounters with the law, from outstanding traffic violations to domestic violence. He'd done this dance before.

Dustin chose another video and showed him. "This is also you purchasing a heater for a hot tub that you used to kill a sweet old lady who never did you any harm."

Jackson again shook his head. "Not me neither. Man, yous got the wrong guy. I didn't kill nobody."

"So, what were you doing in the dark at the Parker house last night?"

"Hey, I'm not say'n 'nother word a'for food. It's like noon. I ain't ate since 'bout now yesterday."

Dustin nodded at Kent, who stepped out the door and retrieved the sack of food and drink. Back inside, he leaned against the closed door, opened the sack, and took an exaggerated sniff. "Breakfast sandwich and hash browns. I've got a drink here too." He shook the cup, rattling the ice.

Kent advanced and slowly pushed the sack and cup toward the young man. Jackson reached for it, clanging the metal restraints on the table. Dustin clamped his hand over the man's tattooed forearm. "Listen, we give, you give. Got it?"

Jackson looked at the food inches away, licked his

lips, and nodded. “I only did a job. That’s all. I ain’t touch nobody.”

“What did you think would happen?”

“I’s only squirt liquid in that plastic pipe. The voice told me what to do. It be his problem. Ask him.”

Dustin removed his hand and Kent gave Jackson the food. He stuffed half the sandwich in his mouth, followed by a gulp of soda.

“Who’s the man with the voice? How’d he hire you?”

With a full mouth, he said, “Long go. A fine watch came along wif a snort, and a Benjamin. I rolled Ben.” He nodded and stuffed the potatoes in his mouth. “A’for I partook, a voice from the watch near scared me to death. I jumped, almost wasted the powder. The voice man said I could get more if I work for him. Say’n light work at night. He pay good too. Yep a few Bens and other niceties come after each gig. But man, I ain’t kill nobody.” Jackson smirked as if he held the keys to all the locks in the jail, bobbed his head to some phantom music, and finished his drink.

“How did you get the liquid for last night?” Dustin leaned in.

“Oh, so that be there a’for.”

“Where?”

“At the address. Always there for me. I show up and what I’s need is there. Voice Man tell me what’a do.”

Dustin’s head swam. How many were involved? “Inside, outside? Where?”

“Depen on job. Most time at entrance.”

“This time?”

He bobbed his head back. “Back door. Found the

needle." He chuckled. "Crawled in doggy door." He pursed his lips, bobbed his head, and scratched his chest. The suspect reminded Dustin of the bobblehead figurines.

Jackson looked at Kent, then Dustin, and held up his hands. "You gonna take these off me?"

Chapter 23

"Two in custody but not the mastermind or the others. How many are there? One did it for money and coke but maintains he didn't lay a hand on the victims. Swears he's innocent. Victoria still insists she hasn't done anything. Do you suppose she was hypnotized?" Dustin leaned back in his chair, fingers interlaced behind his head, and viewed the board.

"That would explain a lot. Is a person guilty under hypnosis?" Kent interjected as Dustin did his out-loud pondering.

He dropped his hands and swiveled toward Kent. "That's unprecedented. Has to be." Dustin stood and flipped his finger on the picture of Doctor Harper. "Doctor?" He flipped his finger on the next image. "Professor?" He rubbed his hand over his mouth and down his cheeks. "Both possess the requisite gray matter. Are they both skilled at hypnotism? We know Doc is and charges people for it."

Dustin took both pictures off the board. "Kent, escort Victoria into interrogation and use wheels. Use your charms and see if she is willing to talk. I'll get a bribe ready."

Kent stood. "Gotcha."

Dustin moved a chair out of the way then plunked down in another one. The door opened and Kent pushed a wheelchair bearing the female into the room. Her sad face and fearful eyes told a story, and he hoped the short confinement opened a window in her brain so information tumbled out. "Good afternoon, Victoria. I hope you've been comfortable as our guest. How is the leg and hand?"

Kent pushed her up to the empty side of the table then sat across next to Dustin. "Comfortable?"

She sighed. "How can I be comfortable locked in a cell when I have a broken leg and some stupid snake bit me? I'm innocent." She frowned and crossed her arms.

Dustin nodded. "Help us out here and we will let the district attorney know that you cooperated." He turned over a picture of Jackson. "Do you recognize this man?"

She stared at the picture. "I don't think so. I want to help, really I do, but he doesn't look familiar."

"Okay. How about this man?" He showed her the grainy video of the masked guy at the pawnshop. "Anything about his body or movements seem familiar?"

Victoria watched the video.

"Get a good look." Dustin replayed it a few times.

"He's skinny like that other guy you showed me but nothing else stands out."

"You're very observant." Dustin smiled.

The door opened and an officer brought in a Styrofoam box and set it on the table.

"Thank you, Officer." The man nodded and left. Dustin slid the box in front of his captive audience. "I understand you eat a healthful diet. Would you like some fresh fruit? Malena handpicked these for you."

"Malena? Is she here?" Hope filled her face as she looked at the closed door.

"She met the officer at the store but sends her love. Go ahead and open it."

Victoria opened the lid. "Oh." A ghost of a smile played across her face as she gazed at a mound of assorted melons, strawberries, grapes, tangerines, and apple pieces.

Kent pulled out a napkin and a plastic fork from his pocket and handed them to her. She accepted it and stabbed a piece of melon.

Dustin noticed the twinkle in his partner's eye. He enjoyed this as much as she did.

The men wore their detective masks, holding in their smiles, giving her time to enjoy half of the offering.

Dustin broke the silence. "How is it? Did Malena guess your favorites?"

Victoria nodded and swallowed. "Yes. The food here isn't too appealing but this is perfect. Good old Mal. She knows me well."

Dustin smiled and swept his hand toward her food. "While you're eating, let me ask you a few questions. Why did you start going to Doctor Harper? Malena told me you endured migraines. Who gave you his name?"

She cocked her head and frowned. "I got his name from an ad in the mail. He sounded too good to be true but I figured what did I have to lose? So I went a few times and it started working. Doctor Harper said I accepted hypnosis well. The migraines vanished and I lost weight, which he denies suggesting, but anyway, I feel great except for the recent events."

"That's fascinating. I'm glad you're over the migraines and I'm sure Malena will help you through the rest."

She ate a few bites.

"Take a look at this guy." Dustin showed her a picture of the professor.

She leaned forward dutifully studying the image. "No. Poor guy. What happened to him?"

"We'll get to that later. How about this one?" He pushed another picture toward her.

"Yes. Why do you have a picture of Noley? I haven't seen him in years. What's he got to do with the mess I'm in?"

"That's the thousand-dollar question. Tell me about him."

"A long time ago, during high school and my freshman year of college, we used to date. We were serious, then a terrible motorcycle accident happened. He got messed up pretty bad. Underwent extensive surgeries and well . . . he changed. Bitterness consumed him. I worried about him and that made me eat too much. You know, comfort food and I gained a ton of weight." She shrugged and sighed.

She scrunched up her face and tears brimmed in her eyes. "He didn't like my added size and I didn't like who he became. I quit visiting him and lost track of his progress."

Kent, always prepared, handed her tissues.

“Thanks.” She hiccupped and dabbed at her tears.

“Did his face get injured?”

“Yes. Fractured cheekbone and nose, and road rash took off most of his skin. He almost lost an eye.” She shuddered.

Dustin put the pictures side by side in front of her. In a moment, she gasped and held a shaky hand over her mouth. “Oh no. They’re the same person. Poor Noley.” The tears spilled in earnest. She cradled her head in her arms on the table and wept.

Back in her cell, Tori sat on the bed and propped her leg on a pillow then stared at the ceiling. She whispered, “God, are You there? Mal said You wouldn’t give me visions of things after the fact. She said You and I may not have a relationship. I don’t understand that. How do I have a relationship with someone so far away? I remember hearing that You needed an invitation to come into my life. Said you are a gentleman and won’t force Your way in. So, Jesus, I want a relationship with You and if I’m supposed to ask, then I ask You to come in. I’m sorry I didn’t ask before and I’m sorry for all the messes I’ve made.” She hiccupped. “The sin in my life.”

Tears slid down her face as joy filled her heart. Incredible love surrounded her like a hug. Heaven wasn’t as far away as she thought. “Is that You Jesus? Did you come in? I feel. . .” Tears soared onto the pillow under her head. She felt like they were part of her cleansing. No matter what happened now, she knew she was loved. God loved her. Peace she'd never experienced calmed her from head to toe. A huge smile spread. Tori looked around the enclosure and her voice raised, "Come what may, I'm now Your child. Thank You, Heavenly Father. Mal was right."

Chapter 24

Arrest and search warrants in hand, Dustin and Kent with several officers arrived to storm Professor George Noland Olson's castle. "After the door opens, prop it so it doesn't close. He controls the locks." Dustin waved at the camera, flashed his badge, and showed the legal document.

In a few minutes, brittle laughter came from the speaker under the camera. "What do you think you'll find, Detective? You're too late. Always a step behind."

The lock clicked and the door opened. A bewildered-looking Lewis, George's brother, waited just inside.

"We have warrants. That means we can come in and search." Dustin gently pushed open the door. "Where is your brother?"

"D-down in b-basement."

Dustin clasped him on his shoulder. "Thank you, Lewis. Don't be frightened. Everything will be all right." The other officers scattered through the house.

Lewis's eyes grew wide as he turned to watch the officers.

Poor guy. He must think we're an invading army. Dustin looked around and saw familiar smoke detectors. Cameras may be hidden in them. He wouldn't put it past the creep to spy on his own family. He nodded to an officer who carried a ladder to uncover and dismantle the cameras. "Is your mother home?"

Lewis nodded and shuffled to another room. Dustin followed him into a large room with bare white walls and a window with the shade drawn. Two lamps lit the space. A small, birdlike woman, whom he knew to be Fran, sat at a immense table with puzzle pieces scattered. Some pieces were locked together into a large frame. She lifted her head and Dustin saw what appeared to be a piece of leather attached across her mouth.

Dustin whispered, "Dang." He ran over to remove it from her. The woman shrank back. Dustin stopped. "Ma'am, can I remove that for you?"

The fear real, Fran looked behind him into the hall.

Dustin reached out and clasped her hand. "George can't hurt you anymore." What kind of monster would do this especially to his own mother?

"M-mom," Lewis squeaked out.

"I believe your son Lewis wants you to let me take it off."

Lewis nodded.

Reaching behind her, Dustin unbuckled the device, being careful not to tug her choppy gray hair, pulling it free. She worked her jaw and rubbed the marks it left. "Thank you," she croaked out and swallowed. "Did George come up?"

He handed her the nearest glass. "Take a drink."

With two shaky hands, she held the glass to her lips and sipped.

A diabolical crackle slashed through the room.

Dustin saw the speaker in the wall. George. Of course, he would watch his family. All about control.

"Sir?"

Dustin recognized Kent's voice and turned to the mother and son. "Excuse me." He pointed at a uniformed officer. "This officer will sit with you." The deputy stayed with them, and Dustin followed Kent down the hall to the elevator.

Kent pointed to the pad beside the elevator door. "We're unable to access it. It's only operated by a handprint. No keypad."

"The tech team not here yet?"

Kent shook his head.

Frustrated, he had hoped they could bypass it with a code. Before he entered the house, he had thought of the possibility of another way. Dustin hurried back to the mother and son. "Do any of your hands open the elevator door?"

Immediate fright etched their faces and both sets of eyes widened in appearance of hard-boiled eggs with small dots in the middle. "G-george ssay no," Lewis whispered in his endearing stutter.

Drat. As he figured. "Don't worry. It will be all right." He patted the child-man's hand that held his mother's then checked his watch. The techs from Denver should've been here by now. Dustin orchestrated this as an all fronts' assault. He needed to assure this tiny abused family. "I promise we won't let him hurt you. We need to talk to him and see the basement where he works. Then we will take him away so he can't hurt you anymore. Can either of you open the door?"

Their bodies shook and they clung together. "He

won't let us in there." Fran croaked out a warning.

Dustin clicked off the phone and whispered to Kent, "The techs will be here ASAP. Traffic. Right now, we need to dust for viable prints in order to trick the fingerprint pad. You'll find the best ones in George's bedroom."

"This w-way." Lewis disentangled himself from his mother and led them down a hall in the opposite direction from the elevator.

Sharp ears. Impressed yet leery with the change in Lewis, Dustin, along with Kent followed.

"I thought the bedrooms were upstairs and accessible outside?"

"Not G-george's."

"Lewis, did your brother put the gag on your mother?"

He shook his head.

"Did he demand you put it on her?"

Lewis's eyes welled up. He tucked his head and squeaked, "Yes."

Dustin patted his shoulder. "Lewis, you and your mom are safe. Thank you for being helpful and answering my questions. You can tell me anything." Poor guy. Servitude to a maniac. Dustin prayed for strength to control his anger when he came face to face with the monster.

A slight nod and with his face toward the floor, Lewis pointed to the double doors. "G-George's room. I can only go in when he tells me. H-he knows. He hears.

He sees."

Dustin breached the lair, opening the French doors wide. On entry, the hairs on the back of his neck stood up. There were cameras mounted on every wall, not hidden this time. At that moment, Professor Olson knew Dustin invaded his domain. He faced the camera, grinned, and saluted him, wishing he could witness the man's reaction.

The immaculate large room contained stark furnishings. Nothing ornate. A forlorn wider-than-normal single sized bed, that could pass a military inspection, sat centered and perpendicular to the white wall, forming a T. A dresser with a mirror straight across on the opposite wall completed the furnishings. Kent dusted for prints.

To give the watcher a taste of his own medicine, Dustin sat for a moment on the bed and untucked the tightly made sheets. Who made it? Lewis? Fran? Next, he opened and riffled inside each drawer in the dresser, paying particular interest in the underwear drawer leaving the contents sticking out. That should make his skin crawl. Did the watcher appreciate the violation? "Right back atcha."

A doublewide doorway led to the bathroom. The wide-open room held equipment for the wheelchair-bound man, complete with a roll-in lounge-type shower chair inside the mega stall. The shower sported jets on all the walls and a waterfall showerhead over top.

Cameras here too. Dustin shuddered.

"Now that you've seen my lair, what do you think, Detective?" George's voice flowed from a speaker set into the wall.

Turning to Kent, Dustin whispered, "Upload those

prints into the computer." Time. It ran too fast. A man's life might end if he didn't get into the elevator. Dustin wanted to bring in the Precision Murderer alive. He couldn't fail. Perspiration glistened on his forehead. Flashing light from his phone drew his attention. The Techs arrived. He rushed to meet them.

A frustrating twenty minutes later, the use of biometric spoofing made access. Fingerprints collected and scanned into the computer were mirrored and arranged into a full hand then printed out. Dustin took the honor of placing the print onto the elevator scanner. The door swooshed open. Dustin let out the breath he didn't know he held. "Thank you, Lord." He, Kent, an EMT, and three officers stepped in and pushed the down button.

Dustin tapped his fingers against his leg as the vault slid down into the bowels of the house. The door whizzed open and he waited for the officers to swarm out and detain the suspect. The EMT went next to ascertain his condition and test for poisons using a ChemSee kit.

Professor George Olson sat in his chair, a slight callous smirk on his face. "We meet again, Detective. A little on the slow side but congratulations on breaching the security on my print reader. Your delay gave me more time with my crew. Welcome to my command station where video and communication take my intellect to a greater dimension."

He turned his hands up, splaying his fingers. "As you can clearly see, there are still ten addresses."

George's hands weren't strapped down and he was much more mobile than portrayed in their earlier meeting. That news smacked Dustin between the eyes.

Did George direct Lewis to bind his arms to the chair as a ruse to divert suspicion from him? The professor almost thought of everything. Almost.

The EMT gave George an injection to counteract whatever poison George ingested, probably cyanide. Unable to stop it, George glared at him then at Dustin.

The EMT nodded. Dustin relaxed. "Well, seems we got here in time. Now, you can't take the coward's way out. You'll face justice after all. Of course, your Maker will have the final word on your life. I pity you."

The professor's face turned stone cold and his eyes reflected steel gray like the hull of a battleship. A storm raged within him.

Dustin estimated the temperature in the twenty by twenty room to be somewhere around a cool sixty-five degrees. A wall held ten rows of monitors all in perfect lines and evenly spaced. A table stood in front of them where the professor sat to survey his diabolical plan in real time. Dustin stepped closer to the ten rows of monitors. Unbelievable. One row showed the rooms of this house. Lewis sat with his mother and an officer stood nearby.

On another line, he recognized the front of his own house and on another monitor, the back. Heat raced up his neck. The creep still watched him. They hadn't found all the cameras. Blank monitors in the same row must be where his team had taken down the other cameras.

Another row clearly displayed the potted flowers on the front porch of Malena's home and on another screen, her sitting room. His heart raced. How dare George invade her privacy? How did they miss these? Dustin glanced back at the madman to read his face and eyes. A confident smirk. Ah. George had replaced them. Today? Why?

Each row held other focuses of a diabolical scheme. Numerous rooms and the outside of Marlow's home. Headquarters? Inside his office? You've got to be kidding. Dustin shook with fury. Doctor Harper ranked his own row which included his therapy room where the unsuspecting victim sat relaxed talking to a patient in a recliner. One seemed to be a storage unit. Victoria Miller rated a row all her own. On other rows he didn't recognize the houses or occupants. Ten. An even number. A whole number.

Dustin searched for names or addresses. A scrap of paper peeked out from under a joystick. He removed it. A list of addresses. For some, a meticulously straight-as-an-arrow line was drawn through. He recognized the addresses, where the dead had been removed in body bags. The demented professor scratched off their residences like a score sheet. Nauseated, Dustin wanted to punch the smirk off Professor George Olson's face.

A line crossed through Victoria's address. He typed a message into his phone. Check on Victoria Miller. Did George have one of their own on the payroll? Cleaning crew at the jail?

Dustin pulled out a set of handcuffs and clamped one side on the Professor and secured it to the chair. "George Noland Olson, you are under arrest for the murder of Colin Raffey, Jane Dixon, Regina Billings, Ted Wilson, Burt Swanson, and Anna Buckingham. Also, the attempted murder of Detective Jim Marlow, Rex and Senna Parker, Victoria Miller, and myself. I'm sure we can slap on a dozen other charges. You have the right to remain silent. Anything you say can and will be held against you in a court of law. You have the right to an attorney. If you cannot afford an attorney, one will be appointed to you."

The professor grunted. "I bet that made you feel good."

"This whole thing sickens me. Are you coming or do we need to carry you out?"

The prisoner twisted the joystick on his motorized chair and headed toward the open elevator.

Chapter 25

"How did you zero in on the professor and figure it out?" Kent asked as he came in from releasing Victoria on bail and handed Dustin a cup of coffee.

"Thanks." Dustin leaned back in his chair and grinned. "Have a seat and I'll tell you. But first—I got the word—the desk is yours. The paperwork came through. You've been assigned a permanent position with me if you'll have it. So, Detective Timothy Kent, welcome aboard." Dustin stood and clasped his friend's hand.

"Thank you, Sir." Kent laughed. "Detective. Ah. Dustin."

"You deserve it, Tim."

Kent grinned, plopped down at his desk and rubbed his hand over the surface, then picked up his coffee cup and took a swig.

Dustin cleared his throat and sat. "I kept thinking about our two larger than life suspects—the ones who could mastermind this mess—and went back through their past lives. Then I came across the accident report and it all made sense."

He swallowed coffee and continued his story. "I was there. My partner and I got the call of an accident."

"First on the scene." Dustin nodded. "I was a green rookie. A car and motorcycle collided. Horrific accident. My partner ran to the truck and I to the flaming bike. I couldn't believe the motorcycle guy was still alive. I found a weak pulse. I called for a bus then pulled him out from under the burning bike and off the road. They told me later I saved his life.

"Anyway, the ironic thing is the driver of the truck got away with a broken arm and a few abrasions, even though they used the Jaws of Life to extract him. The crushed truck rolled a few times before coming to rest against a tree."

He shook his head at the memory. "There's no telling how fast he drove around the curves. Earlier, he'd been drinking and that's probably why he didn't sustain much damage. He claimed a deer ran out in front of him and he swerved."

Dustin stared off at the blank wall, remembering. "The ambulances sped the injured to the hospital, my partner and I checked out the accident scene, and it turned out he told the truth. We found a wounded doe fifty feet off the road. The animal lost a leg and sustained other damage. My partner put her down.

"I wrote up the report but got called out on a search and rescue mission in the mountains and much to my chagrin, I didn't follow up on either of the injured." Dustin hung his head in regret for a moment.

"The truck driver got a slap on the wrist, cleaned up his act, went to medical school, and became the frustrating Doctor Fredrick Harper who now specializes in hypnotism.

"The motorcycle guy whose life I saved, and Victoria identified as Noley, is Professor George

Noland Olson."

Kent whistled. "Any idea why he was bent on so much mayhem?"

Lacing his hands behind his head, Dustin leaned back creating the familiar creek in his chair. "My best guess is revenge. He targeted Harper's patients, therefore putting the doctor in our suspect pool. Somehow, he came up with this incredible way to get people to do his bidding. Using a two-way communication device is masterful. He took Harper's claim to fame—hypnotism—which also pointed to the doctor as the culprit. He hypnotized others to deliver devices, break in homes, plant cameras, and kill because he couldn't do it himself."

Kent leaned forward resting his elbows on his knees, still holding his cup. "Yes. Continue."

"Then he mailed Victoria the flyer that sent her running to his enemy, Doctor Harper."

"Ah, right." Kent smiled and finished off his drink.

"From monitoring the doctor's therapy room, the evil professor figured out who hypnotism worked best on and paid off others, creating his squad of workers. He maintained a storage unit where we found more creatures and their food supplies. We also found electronics, watches, and other equipment, so much evidence for the D.A. to build their case.

"His minions were the key. He didn't use one person but multiple players. Victoria delivered things to the addresses. Jackson Black did the actual killing, even though he didn't touch anyone as he so eloquently proclaimed, and Steven Holms supplied what Victoria took to the kill sites. Holms may be instrumental as a carrier pigeon of mail and other such seemingly innocent objects as Victoria is.

Then there's our fellow guard, Gary, who took the bribe and administered the narcotics into her drink. Timing on our part and seeing her name scratched off the list saved her life. Gary told Victoria the special drink came from Malena. Of course, that never happens in jail. Anyway, it's a good thing she didn't like it and only took a tiny sip."

Anger flashed across Kent's features. "I hope the judge throws the book at him."

"He'll get his." Dustin nodded and rubbed a hand over his face. Would he ever catch up on sleep?

His partner took a deep breath, visibly calming himself. "Speaking of Tori, do you think the Professor hypnotized her to lose weight? She said the doc didn't do it."

Dustin still harbored a distrust of the good doctor but agreed the professor took advantage. "Probably. She said, back in the day, Noley didn't like her added weight. Besides, she'd be more agile to do his bidding. Did you know she recently changed her hair color? Malena told me she used to be a blonde. That may have been one of his suggestions through hypnotism to her. I believe he did it as a test to see how much control over her he wielded."

"Reasonable assumption. He may've garnered the satisfaction of playing god over her to that extent. I feel sorry for Tori because she didn't do anything on purpose. She doesn't have a memory of any of it." Kent crossed his arms.

"I hear ya buddy. This case, when it became clear that Victoria, or Tori as you and Malena call her, was deep into it, has been hard on you. You acted as an officer of the law should even though from the first, Tori caught your attention in a romantic way. We have to put our feelings in a box and put that box on a shelf too high to reach until it's all over. Take a deep breath, my friend. I think the judge will be lenient because of what you just said. She didn't know what she was doing."

"Hope you're right. I'm going to put in a good word, stating she cooperated from the first. She was a victim too. He used her and then made her drive herself into that oak tree. Thank God she didn't get killed. She also paid with the broken leg and the snake venom."

Dustin shivered and nodded. "He directed his diabolical sights on me too. Maybe because I never visited him in the hospital or maybe I injured him more by pulling him from under the motorcycle? Or perhaps he's bitter I saved his life." Dustin shrugged. "Whatever the reason, he came after my partner, my friend Ted, then toyed with Malena, and finally hit me directly with the invasion." He shivered.

Kent chuckled. "Sorry."

"Laugh all you want about the snakes. They are killers. *Killers* Sometime, I might tell you about my first encounter with one."

The End

Here is a chapter from the first book in this series, *Mayhem and Murder in Durango.*

Race of Her Heart

Chapter 1

Confetti spilled as Jalyn opened the card. Grinning, she read the words.

Hope you had a happy birthday.
It will be your last!

The card slipped from her fingers and she sank to her knees. Covering her face in her hands, a moan escaped. She wiped the moisture from her cheeks. Her hands shook as she picked up miniature metallic skull and crossbones.

Somehow she managed to get to her couch and made a call.

"This is Jalyn Stewart I need to report another incident…Yes…Yes, you do…Correct…Please hurry…"

She hugged a pillow as the world around her shrunk and the worry and fear from last year came back in waves.

A knock at the door sent her to peer out the peephole. An officer and a badge. She opened, leaving the chain hooked to scrutinize her caller before sliding it out of the way.

"Miss Stewart, remember me? Officer Kent, and this is Detective Marlow."

"Thank you for coming. It's there." She pointed to the mess on the floor of her new digs back in her home town of Durango.

The officer pulled on gloves and stooped to gather the evidence.

Detective Marlow said, "I spoke to Detective

Green who handled your case in Lake Placid. He's sending me the file. We'll get to the bottom of this. Officer Kent will be in the loop and you can contact either of us. We take care of our own. Let us know if you get any more threats."

Jalyn shook their hands, they departed and she double-locked the door. She didn't want this latest incident to rule over her mind and emotions. She squared her shoulders and raised her chin.

The next few weeks became a whirl of activity as she tried to keep herself busy, pushing the thought of the birthday warning out of her mind. Although she kept a watchful eye and glanced frequently over her shoulder.

You thought moving here would make you safe.

The doorframe yielded the scrap of paper at the first tug. Jalyn reread the note and again the words jumped off the page. Her stomach dropped.

A frown creased her forehead and her heart thumped as she entered her apartment and leaned against the door. "Why does this keep happening?" she whispered to an empty room. The eerie words mocked her. A psycho had her in his crosshairs. The keys clanged onto the table along with the note.

The deadline loomed. Jalyn imagined crumpled paper balls strewn on her floor around the worn desk, had she used a typewriter instead of her computer. Her part-time job took more hours than she had anticipated when she hired on eight months ago but she had embraced and enjoyed her journalist position. Her boss, Clark, although a taskmaster, had been a family friend for years. He hired her for her sports interests in both baseball and skiing and for her hometown roots. Jalyn's journalist classes helped with the technical aspects, but he seemed to love the insight and passion she wrote in her posts and as a bonus allowed her to work from home. All in all, moving back to Durango from Lake Placid had been a blessing.

Writing about the events in the town of her birth brought her face to face with the people and their uplifting or sad stories and she loved the connection.

Lately, though, she found it difficult to focus on the happenings of Durango, Colorado. Preparations for the upcoming race and parade didn't seem important. Planning her wedding—that was important.

The office chair squeaked as she leaned back. Jalyn's eyes went to the padded green memo board she had made with blue ribbon held on with dark blue daisy pushpins. The fun board held reminders and special keepsakes slid in under the thin ribbon. Pictures of her parents, a picture with her in ski clothes and skis ready to push off down the slopes, a dried rose from Timothy hung upside down, and a card that said, "Save the Date" all caught her eye. At the top of the card, a photograph showed Timothy with his arm around her, their joined hands resting on his thigh. Seated on a huge fallen tree, they were surrounded by breathtaking orange, yellow, and golden leaves. Below, a caption announced, *Timothy Blake and Jalyn Stewart are getting hitched!* A bold red circle appeared on the small calendar denoting, *Saturday, September 24.*

She grinned at the remembered moment almost two years ago. Love and happiness. So much had happened since that picture including her skiing accident last year and recovery. Jalyn loved the picture and would have been happy with this being the only invitation but the formal white and gold ones were waiting to be mailed. She had spent hours folding and stuffing them. Timothy had wanted her to have the printers do everything but Jalyn wanted to save money.

Another cup of coffee should boost her drive. The kitchenette a few feet away held her coffee bar which included a fancy drip pot, flavorings, sweeteners, cream, and cups hung on a rack on the wall under the cupboard. The grinder hummed as she stretched, relieving the kinks in her neck and back, and the throbbing in her leg. Brilliant sunlight from outside sparkled off her chrome coffeepot.

Sounds from the bustling street below beckoned her to the open window. Colorful flowers arrayed in pots, banners strung across Main Street, and a sizzle of excitement filled the spring air. The historic town that melded into contemporary, geared up for the first motorized bicycle race vs. steam engine. The route would take them on an exciting 45.2 mile journey—traversing the tracks and up Highway 550 through Animas Valley in the heart of the San Juan Mountains, a three-thousand foot incline in elevation up to Silverton, an old mining town turned tourist stop.

Jalyn's mind went to the article she wrote a few days ago. History marked races of all sorts—dirt bike, foot, car, and even mule back in the day, but this was unique. Not that electric bicycles were new, they'd been invented in the 1880s, or so the research for her article explained. This race idea started as a bet on the mighty steam engine to rule supreme. Two means brought travelers to Silverton—highway and train. The people of La Plata County would soon find out the true champion and crown their victor.

A chime alerted Jalyn as the nutty aroma reached her senses. Anticipating the flavor, she smiled. "Ahh, coffee." The first sip—magical. Mug in hand, she reclaimed her place before the computer. Coffee close and available for short interruptions, her fingers flew across the computer keyboard and click-clicked for the next half hour.

The screen blinked, message sent. She grinned, satisfied she finished before deadline and hoped Clark, her editor, would be happy with her piece. Jalyn stood and stretched, touched her toes, and then reached high above her head. She scooted her chair under the desk, traversed the few feet to place her cup in the dishwasher, grabbed her handbag, and rushed out to her first wedding dress fitting.

The little boutique beckoned a passerby to stop and view the window display of gorgeous gowns and tempt a bride-to-be to walk in to try on a new or handmade gown or have alterations made. She smiled as the bell above the door announced her arrival. "Old-fashioned-Chic" was how she would describe the atmosphere and wares.

Malena Campbell, her best friend and seamstress, greeted her with a hug. "Finish the deadline?"

Jalyn grinned. "In the hands of Clark as we speak."

"Yay! Now you can relax and slip into your

gown." Malena guided her to the dressing room.

In a few moments, Jalyn stood in a creamy white dress.

Malena regarded her and winked. "You chose well, Jalyn. The ivory complements your complexion, and contrasts nicely with your auburn hair. Your blue eyes sparkle. Give me a turn so we can catch the swish of your dress."

Jalyn did as bidden, stopped, and studied herself and her friend in the mirror. Delighted smiles filled both ladies' faces. Malena met her gaze and gathered material at her waist. "I'll take a tuck here to accentuate your curves. Where do you want the hem? Did you find the shoes you'll be wearing?"

"Oh, no! I forgot to order them." In the mirror, Jalyn caught her friend's eyes focusing on the trademark of stress in her life—a one-sided smirk. With purpose, she relaxed her expression.

Malena mumbled through pins in her mouth, "That's all right, I'll do the altering and later we can hem. Let me know when you're free after your shoes arrive." She removed the last pin and secured it through the fabric. "Is Colleen styling your hair and makeup?"

"Yes. I'm grateful she moved here shortly after I did. Having a professional makeup artist and hairdresser who worked with me before is a wonderful gift. We had an enjoyable time searching sites and deciding on a hair style. I chose an upsweep creation with a few loose ends. She suggested sparkly pins scattered throughout, which will enhance my jewelry."

Malena smiled at Jalyn's reflection. "The image is striking."

Jalyn watched as Malena frowned and scanned her

features. She felt the scrutiny and resisted the urge to look down. Instead, she met her friend's eyes.

"Are you relaxing this evening or is there a game?" Malena asked.

"I'm umping two—at six, and eight o'clock."

"I don't know how you do all the physical things you do. Running down leads for stories and umping baseball and softball. How is your leg?"

"You know. Stiff and sore. The splintered bones ripped up the muscles and the plate gets cold sometimes. Nothing some heat cream, hot baths, and pain meds can't cure. Push through the pain, right? Don't worry, I'm fine."

"You would tell me if you weren't?"

Jalyn slipped her arm across her friend's shoulders. "Of course. BFF's do that."

Malena grinned and nodded. "Yep. Since high school." She crossed her arms. "I thought you had a date with Timothy."

"He canceled. He's working on a brief for court. And as it happens, they were short umpires so I took the extra two games."

Malena pursed her lips. "Timothy should be pleased you have the added income."

"Don't be mean. He just thinks I need to stay busy."

Malena rolled her eyes. "Right."

Jalyn caught the look and let her shoulders slump. Sadness clambered to take possession of her soul. Malena and Jalyn didn't see eye to eye when it came to Timothy and what Malena perceived as his lack of attention and assumed motives. Would Malena retract her inference? Jalyn swiveled and gazed at Malena, hoping.

Instead, Malena changed the subject. “Are you going to the singles’ pizza party Saturday?”

So again, this was how it was going to be. Stuffing down her sadness Jalyn answered, “I’m not sure. Clark wants me to cover the cyclists’ arrival. The racers are here three weeks early to get acclimated and familiarize themselves to the route. They’re scheduled to arrive on the bus at two. You know, all the hoopla and fan-fare. Afterward, I head home to write it up for Sunday’s edition.”

“Party’s not until seven. Why don’t you invite those participating in the race? The cute ones, at least. It’s good for morale,” Malena wiggled her eyebrows.

“Yours, maybe.” Jalyn grinned at her best friend, deciding not to stay upset. Malena had a right to her opinion and they had been friends since they were children. “I’ll choose the best-looking one without a ring on his finger and ask him if he is interested in making an acquaintance of a tall brunette. Will that do?”

Malena chuckled and hugged her, “You know, I love you and I trust you to pick out the cutest one.”

Jalyn winked and dashed in the other room to change into her umps uniform.

Jalyn arrived early to the ball fields. She called the games without an overabundance of complaints from the players or hecklers in the stands. Too many times, the adult players acted like children, argued, grumbled, and sometimes tossed the bat with a force to rival a cannon ball. She umped different leagues, all ages, on various days. One of the children's teams had a difficult coach. Kicking dirt on her became a normal occurrence.

A few days ago, she had a run-in with Coach Reid. He didn't like the strike-out call she'd made. The large man got in her face and wouldn't let up. He screamed and kicked dirt. "Blind woman! Anyone with any sense could see that the ball was inside. Heck! It could have hit my player! Were you napping again?" When the obscenities flew, she ejected him. The other coach had to encourage him off the field. Reid fumed and mumbled that he'd get even with her. She tried to shrug it off. Boys will be boys, even six-foot-two, handsome, and when not on the ball diamond, charming and gregarious.

When she got home, she drew a bath and added Epsom salts. The hot water eased her sore muscles and throbbing leg. As she soaked, she opened a book and stretched out, resting her head on a blue and green air pillow adhered with suction cups to the porcelain. She loved to relax and read in a tub of hot water to ease the soreness, especially at the end of taxing days. Today was especially taxing. Working the extra games exacted weariness and pain on her bones and muscles and the body language and verbiage of Coach Reid bothered her. Anytime she called a ruling against one of his players he seethed and fussed at her. She took her job serious and like the other day, the ball had clearly crossed in the strike zone. A foul was still a foul, a clean tag couldn't be called anything other than an out.

The novel should've been a good distraction but she couldn't concentrate. She finally set it aside. The conversation with Timothy played again in her mind. "Jalyn, I need to work and can't take you out to dinner and a movie. We'll need to make it another time."

"Oh, Timothy, I've been looking forward to your company and the movie. I hear it's got crazy action. Are you sure?"

"Tell you what, how about breakfast tomorrow morning at the diner, eight o'clock? I really need to work. I'm sorry to disappoint."

"Eight it is. I'll miss you."

"Yeah. See you tomorrow."

"Love you."

Nothing. She had spoken to an ended call. He had already hung up. Not even a good-bye. Jalyn went deeper into the water, up over her chin. He spent way too much time at the office.

After toweling off and donning her comfy purple cotton jammies, she crashed on the sofa for a movie, enjoyed a salad, and grabbed her computer to order a pair of adorable pumps to go with her wedding gown. Her phone chimed near the close of the movie. Not wanting the interruption, she let it go to voicemail.

Saturday morning's sunlight brought Jalyn up early. She chose her clothes carefully. The breeze warned of a cooler temperature and she needed to dress the part of a reporter. Blue denim vest on top of cream pullover, jeans, heels, and a bold splash of coral statement jewelry. A little bit of sophistication, but not too much, for this mountain town. The day, she anticipated, would be busy.

Jalyn's stomach rumbled as she anticipated the peace offering breakfast. She walked the few blocks to the café, hoping Timothy had made reservations. At this time of year, the town teemed with tourists so she never knew if a table would be available.

As she stopped at a light, she glanced at her cell, and remembered she'd neglected to check her messages. The call she didn't answer last night had a blocked number, but a message had been left. "You were lucky," the muffled voice warned.

Jalyn froze as icy fingers gripped her heart. She instinctively glanced around, and then frowned at her phone. She whispered, "Why is this happening? Who is this psycho?" Unwilling to let this creep take over her life by inciting fear, she kept walking. It took her a block to steady her nerves. Timothy would think her childish, and she could imagine his reaction. "Jumping at shadows, dear. A misdial. Happens all the time." A tinge of guilt from keeping this all to herself clambered for attention. All her problem, not anyone else's. She tugged at her vest, and straightened her shoulders before pulling open the door to the café.

Always on time, if not early, he looked handsome wearing a dark burgundy open neck pullover and jeans, his brown hair combed to perfection. Gray eyes met hers, and a smile spread showing a great wall of pearly whites. He stood and pulled out the empty chair, giving her a kiss on her cheek before she sat.

"Jalyn, you look beautiful today, an important meeting?"

One eyebrow shot up. "I thought I mentioned it. I'm covering the arrival of the racers this afternoon."

He picked up his menu and shook his head. "I'm sure you didn't."

She held her menu without seeing it, as she remembered back to their conversation a few days ago.

His voice in her head as clear as it was then. *"I hope you get a bonus for acting as a reporter instead of your normal pay for an article."*

"My title is journalist, Timothy. That means, if they want me on a story, I go—extra pay or not."

"That might be fine this summer, but don't let him take advantage of you next season when you're a ski instructor to the elite." He had winked, but his words still stung.

Her favorite server, Delores, came to the table which brought Jalyn to the present, and they gave her their choices from the menu. "I'll be right back with your coffee."

Jalyn and Timothy didn't say anything as they waited. Delores returned and poured the rich dark liquid into their cups, smiled, and went to another table. Jalyn added a bit of cream and a sweetener. The coffee soothed as it warmed her. She smiled at Timothy, dispelling her disappointment in his forgetfulness. "Coffee is good this morning."

"Ah, huh."

"I tried on my dress for our wedding. Malena has to take it in a little."

"Hum."

"I ordered the cutest shoes."

"Okay."

Their omelets arrived with side of fruit for her and a bran muffin for him. They bowed their heads in a silent prayer, and turned their concentration to the meal.

Her mind went to a time when he used to converse with more than guttural answers. His mind must be on the case. "Are you going to the singles pizza hangout tonight?"

"You know those things don't appeal to me."

"I think I'll go. Malena and Colleen will be there."

"Might as well, while you can. We'll be married soon, and then you won't be tempted to hang out with those *singles* anymore."

Jalyn studied him and felt her eyebrow rise. She almost asked if he meant her friends or the group. Instead, she changed the subject and relaxed her brow. "Are you coming to Mom's after church for lunch?"

"I have to work. I need to get more research finished before the court case. I need to button it up, patch up some loopholes, and prepare my opening statement."

Jalyn frowned. "I thought you had your opening ready."

"Oh, I… tore it up. I want to start over with a different punch."

That seemed odd.

After a moment she took a deep breath and said, "Mom's making your favorite, roast with all the fixings, and pie for dessert. I thought it'd be a good time to discuss plans for the wedding and finalize the invitation list."

"Sorry. Have fun without me. You and your mom can enjoy some girl time. Maybe you could bring me a piece of pie on your way home?"

She gazed into his eyes, trying to understand what he might be thinking.

He shifted and signaled for more coffee. "Thanks, Delores. As usual, the coffee is perfect. Can I have a to-go cup please?" He regaled Delores with his charming grin.

I wish he would flirt with me like he used to. Guess

he doesn't feel like he needs to woo me. After all, we're engaged. Still...

"You're far away. Come back to the present."

Jalyn refocused. "Sorry."

"Are you ready? Want to walk with me back to the office?"

She smiled. "Sure."

The café teemed with people. Jalyn wove through the waiting patrons as Timothy followed.

Once outside, he took her hand as they ambled down the street. Her limp wasn't so pronounced and uncomfortable at this pace. He matched her progress. "I'm sorry this case is taking so much of my time."

"I understand you have a job to do, and you're a wonderful attorney. That's one of the things I love about you—your passion for what you do." She rested her head against his shoulder.

"Don't hold a seat for me at church. I'll be working all day."

She stopped and looked up at him. "Oh, Timothy. Can't you at least come for the worship service?"

"I moved here when you did, to take this partnership for our future. I need to make my mark in this town and courtroom. I'll have more time after this case."

They started off again and soon arrived at his office. On the door, *Schmitt and Blake* stood out in black lettering. Her fingers traced the name Blake. She smiled at him. "I guess the boss has to show the rest how it's done. After this win, will you be able to hire a paralegal to do the grunt work?"

"I'm hoping to. If we win."

"You will. I have every confidence in you. Also,

I'm praying for your wisdom on this case."

He leaned in, kissed her cheek, and then went inside.

She turned toward her apartment, glanced at her cell phone to check the time, and saw she missed a call from Clark. In a sudden rush, she ducked into the *Durango Herald's* office.

Clark appeared busy as ever, but when he noticed her through the glass, he waved her into his cluttered office. He thumbed to the chair on the other side of his deck. "Take a load off. Great job on the piece. The people will eat it up. Nice bit about that guy who used his electric bicycle to help the people get coal and food after the flood in 1911. That ties in perfectly to our racing characters. Who would have thought electric bikes were invented that long ago?

"Anyway, I still have that staff reporter opening. I could use you fulltime and your presence would give us a little charm around this old building. Whatcha say?"

"Clark." She crossed her arms. "I already told you, tutoring on the slopes gets me as close as I can to my lost Olympic dream, and in the summer I enjoy umping." She nodded. "Besides, I like to keep the pressure down to the bi-monthly deadline." She gave him a toothy grin.

"Okay, kid. Just don't go hurting yourself again." He winked. "You're irreplaceable."

She met his eyes, relieved for the zillionth time pity wasn't evident. "Is there anything else? I need to get to the ball field."

"No. Shoo!" He waved her out the door. "Don't be late meeting the bus! I want an impactful story!"

A few blocks took her to her apartment, situated

over a stitchery and yarn shop, where she threw on her umps uniform. She hurried to her car for the short drive to the ball diamond. Two games later, she dashed back home for a shower and to change back into her outfit to meet the bus.

Parking could be a challenge. She spied a slot. Relieved, she slipped her car in the opening. Jalyn glanced at the digital clock on her dash. The bus should arrive in about ten minutes, if it wasn't late. She grabbed her bag before exiting her vehicle for the short trek.

At the stop, she stood apart, yet near the other people who had gathered. Pieces of conversation drifted toward her. Excited family members waited eagerly for the bus. A few friends or family members hung out to gather their loved one from the bus. Curious townspeople mingled around the bus stop, which meant they had read her article. Jalyn smiled. Phone in hand, she captured a few shots and took mental notes to add another dimension of human interest to her article.

On time, the bus came into view. The hiss of brakes filled the air. The door opened and a slightly rotund man stepped down to open the baggage compartment. He hefted bags not so gingerly to the ground. Passengers disembarked, one at a time. Some had come for a visit, spotting loved ones enthusiastically waving, and rushed over for an embrace.

Jalyn's attention was drawn to an older mother and obvious daughter in an emotional hug. Embarrassed to be caught witnessing the reunion, she turned toward the bus.

Recognition hit her. The handsome face—straight

nose below green penetrating eyes above a quirky mouth with full lips yielded a craggy smile. Her heart lurched. She had last seen him boarding a train five years ago.

Strong broad shoulders on a six-foot, three-inch frame—taller than the other men climbing out who must be contenders for the upcoming race. Most of the men milling about were shorter and very lean. Adam's gaze pierced into her being as realization ignited his face into a contagious lopsided grin. Jalyn couldn't help herself. Giddiness quivered down her spine.

He always did that to her. She had mourned their lost love for a little over two years until she had met Timothy. An impromptu thought crept in. *Had he changed?*

The crowd pressed in, blocking her view. A sudden coolness gave her goose bumps. She rubbed her covered arms. Strange. The sun stood bright in the sky.

Excitement filled the cramped space where the cyclists stood after leaving the bus. The town was absolutely captivated over the race. People advanced for autographs. The three week build-up of excitement would boost interest in the race and the readership of the *Herald*. Also, this gave them plenty of time to mingle with the citizens of Durango and for some to take advantage of the surrounding beauty and sightseeing opportunities.

Jalyn realized she'd shirked her duties and pushed forward. The contestants pulled their dismantled bikes out of the storage under the bus. She punched record on her phone. Avoiding the tall one, she stopped one of the contestants. "Excuse me, I'm Jalyn Stewart from the *Durango Herald*. Can I ask you a few questions?"

"Sure."

"What's your name? When did you get interested in electric bicycles, and is this your first race?"

The questions and answers began as she interviewed the racers. The task unavoidable, she sidled up to Adam Walker. "I didn't know you were coming. I mean, I didn't know you would be one of the contestants."

"Jalyn, you're as beautiful as I remember. Can we go somewhere to talk?"

Dear reader,

I hope you enjoyed this detective whodunit, *See You in 48.* This is my first attempt at writing in this genre and I trust I shined enough light in the midst of the darkness. The bad guy exhibits the depravity of humankind's heart so my desire was to sprinkle love throughout the story. God's loving light will penetrate the blackest heart. If you want to talk about this book or you have questions about any of the topics, please send me a message.

Reviews are essential to authors and I would appreciate it if you would take the time and write a review of *See You in 48.* It doesn't need to be long. A few sentences are great.

Blessings from a fellow traveler of the imagination,

Robin Densmore Fuson

Author Photo: Jamie Herrera Photography @JamieHerreraPhotography

Robin Densmore Fuson is a woman whose main focus is on Christ. As an author and speaker, she shares her passion for truths from God's word and encourages people in their Christian walk. An Amazon best seller, her work has received awards in multiple genres. She and her husband live in Florida with their Belgian Malinois, Kenzi. They celebrate with an overflowing cup of blessings with seventeen grandchildren. Robin loves company and challenges her young guests to discover giraffes in the obvious and hidden nooks and crannies of their home. Her devotions, both written and video, along with book reviews, and flash fiction are on her website. Also, well over a hundred stories for children on kidbiblelessons.

Robin's Website

Books by Robin Densmore Fuson include:

Christian Historical Fiction:
Worthless to Priceless
Romantic Suspense:
Race of Her Heart
Detective Crime:
See You in 48
Allegory Speculative Fiction:
Interruption
Historical Romance and Suspense:
The Dress Shop, Lasso Love, Gamble on Fate, Reflection in Glass,
Contemporary Romance:
Etching in the Snow, Sparkle of Silver
Romantic Christian Women's Fiction:
The Encounter, Restoration
Christmas Romance:
Christmas Inheritance, Christmas Muddle,
Children grade 3-6 Chapter Book Series:
Rosita Valdez and the Giant Sea Turtle, Rosita Valdez and the Attic's Secrets, Rosita Valdez and the Spanish Doll

Robin's Books
on Amazon

Visit her on these sites:

Robin Densmore Fuson: http://www.robindensmorefuson.com/

Blog, Kid Bible Lessons: http://www.kidbiblelessons.com/

Amazon Author Page: https://www.amazon.com/Robin-Densmore-Fuson/e/B06XGKVDDV/ref

Twitter: https://twitter.com/RobinLFuson

FaceBook: https://www.facebook.com/AuthorRobinDensmoreFuson/

Instagram: https://www.instagram.com/robindensmorefuson/

YouTube: (2) Robin Densmore Fuson - YouTube

Pinterest: (12) Pinterest Each book has a board

Goodreads: https://www.goodreads.com/author/show/6604786.Robin_Densmore_Fuson

BookBub:

https://www.bookbub.com/profile/robin-densmore-fuson

Linkedin: Robin Densmore Fuson | LinkedIn

MeWe: (34)MeWe - The Next-Gen Social Network

Alignable: Your Profile (alignable.com)

Made in the USA
Middletown, DE
11 August 2024

58532192R00126